ONE YEAR
in COAL
HARBOR

ONE YEAR
in COAL
HARBOR

POLLY HORVATH

A YEARLING BOOK

Author's Note

Although a real Coal Harbour exists, the town in this book and *Everything on a Waffle* is fictitious.
Canadians call their one-dollar coin a loonie and their two-dollar coin a toonie.
The Royal Canadian Mounted Police, most commonly referred to in speech as the RCMP,
is the Canadian national police service.

Text copyright © 2012 by Polly Horvath
Cover art copyright © 2012 by Aimee Sicuro

All rights reserved. Published in the United States by
Yearling, an imprint of Random House Children's Books, a division of
Random House LLC, a Penguin Random House Company, New York.
Originally published in hardcover in the United States by Schwartz & Wade Books,
an imprint of Random House Children's Books, New York, in 2012.

Yearling and the jumping horse design are registered trademarks of Random House LLC.

Visit us on the Web! randomhouse.com/kids

Educators and librarians, for a variety of teaching tools, visit us at RHTeachersLibrarians.com

The Library of Congress has cataloged the hardcover edition of this work as follows:
Horvath, Polly.
One year in Coal Harbor/Polly Horvath.—1st ed.
p. cm.
Summary: In a small fishing village in British Columbia, twelve-year-old Primrose tries
to be a matchmaker for her Uncle Jack, befriends Ked, a new foster child, tries to decide if she is willing
to go to jail for her convictions, and together with Ked, publishes a cookbook to raise money for the
Fisherman's Aid. Includes recipes.
ISBN 978-0-375-86970-9 (trade) — ISBN 978-0-375-96970-6 (glb) —
ISBN 978-0-375-98536-2 (ebook)
[1. Eccentrics and eccentricities—Fiction. 2. Interpersonal relations—Fiction.
3. Foster home care—Fiction. 4. Family problems—Fiction. 5. Self-reliance—Fiction.
6. British Columbia—Fiction.] I. Title.
PZ7.H79224On 2012
[Fic]—dc23
2011023591

ISBN 978-0-385-38653-1 (pbk.)

Printed in the United States of America

First Yearling Edition 2014

Random House Children's Books supports the
First Amendment and celebrates the right to read.

For Keena and my father

CONTENTS

CONTENTS

What Happened to Quincehead

I WAS SITTING WITH Bert and Evie. Evie had their cockapoo, Quincehead, on her lap and was staring into space. Bert was absently patting Quincehead on the head and rhythmically stroking his back while he told me what had happened.

"This morning when we woke up Quincehead's stomach was huge. Bloated."

"Too big," said Evie.

"Not normal big," said Bert.

"Because sometimes when they eat too much, it gets big," said Evie.

"You can tell easier with little dogs like Quincehead."

"It shows more."

"The big dogs don't show so much."

"Not that we ever had a big dog."

"'Cause we haven't."

"I prefer a dog that can sit in my lap."

"We always get Evie lapdogs."

"So," they said together as if this were a logical pausing place in their narrative.

I waited patiently. They were looking out the window at the storm with unseeing eyes. The rain poured down and the wind howled. It was probably the last real winter blow.

The storm had started that morning. We had been able to hear the surf even in our classes at school, pounding the shore, flinging spray.

I had been sitting in class thinking that when the earth shakes like this, what you need is some solid ground beneath your feet, such as the bedrock of multiplication, where if you multiply correctly, you always get the same sum. But one look outside tells you how it is all just an invention in the end. What do we really know? Everything we know is just something someone made up. I like to cook, and you would think one of cooking's reassuring aspects would be that if you make the same recipe the same way, it always comes out the same. This would be a nice antidote to random events if what you always wanted was a peach melba. But anyone who cooks a lot can tell you that it is hogwash. You can make the same recipe the same way a dozen times and each time it comes out differently. There are whole days when everything you cook comes out terribly and others when you can do no wrong. So many factors you will never be aware of are involved. Anyone who thinks they've got it all scoped out is in for a few surprises.

I'd nudged Eleanor, who sits next to me, and continued this thought out loud. "So if you're going to make something up, you might as well make sure it is something good. Just like if you don't know what is going to happen and have to assume, you might as well assume something good."

She'd looked at me blankly. She hates it when I nudge and whisper during class, even though our teacher, Miss Connon, is extremely tolerant. Miss Connon doesn't mind the odd communication while she's talking, and she reads us essays by people like Walt Whitman and Mary Oliver because she credits us all with at least as much intelligence as we have. I could see Eleanor turning to look out the window and her brow furrowing again as she thought about what I'd said. I know mine is just one way of seeing things. That this was what I saw in the storm. I'd been hoping, as always, for a meeting of the minds but she just whispered, "Oh, great, indoor gym again."

I'd turned back to watch the ocean. It looked like the sea was flinging bedsheets over a bed that refused to stay made. It could not make the sheets lie flat and neat and tidy. Waves bunched up and wrinkled and lifted high into the air to be flung across their sea beds once more. Order and disorder, order and disorder, I'd thought, staring out the window until Miss Connon called on me. That snapped me to, and looking down at my textbook to answer her question, I'd realized that the last time I had looked at my book we were still on math but it turned out they had moved on to Canadian history and the settling of the plains. Miss Connon turned tactfully to someone else while I switched books and caught up. We were now apparently talking about the Doukhobors, who walked naked across Saskatchewan. "We all live in uncertainty, and people will do amazing things in their need to get a grip, even, it would seem, naked protest parades," said Miss Connon.

I'd drifted back to the window and wondered if my father, who is a fisherman, had docked his boat yet or had come in early before the storm started. I was a little concerned because the previous year he and my mother had been lost at sea during a bad winter storm. So I'd been relieved when after school I met up with my father, still dressed in his fishing gear and carrying a salmon home for us. I had waved, called out I was going to Bert and Evie's and trotted on. I don't tell him that I still worry every time his fishing boat goes out. I don't want him to worry that I worry. After all, what can he do? This is how he makes a living.

Bert and Evie had been my foster parents for a short time when my parents were lost at sea. By the time my parents returned, Bert and Evie and I were like a small family unit, so it was very unsettling for them to find me leaving for another family, even if that family was my own. The previous night they had called to say I should drop by after school. They might have some good news. But now, here I was, and instead they told me about Quincehead.

"So we took him to the vet," said Bert. "We told the vet we thought he had eaten something bad. You know how he eats anything."

"He's like a shark. Anything in his path. Once he ate a whole tableful of bread dough I had left to rise." Evie said this while looking dully out into a world that would soon contain no such feats of appetite.

"That's how we found out he could get up on chairs."

"So this morning the vet examined him. But . . ."

"It wasn't something he ate. It was cancer," said Bert.

"I didn't know dogs could get cancer," I said. I have a dog named Mallomar who my uncle Jack bought for me last year to help take my mind off the fact that everyone thought my parents were dead. But Mallomar is young and healthy so I had had no run-ins with dog diseases yet.

"You don't ever anticipate all the bad things that can happen," said Evie. "If we did we would never get through a day. Not a single day."

"Yep, there's diseases both dogs and people can have," said Bert.

"But not colds. Dogs can't catch your colds, so you don't have to worry about sneezing on them."

"But they *do* get some of the same diseases," said Bert.

"Cancer, for one," said Evie.

"It's his spleen. That's why he's so blown up like that. The vet said he didn't have much time left."

"I asked how much time. I was thinking, like months or years even."

"But it was hours. The vet said the kind thing would be to put him down immediately right there in the office. Right that minute. But Evie couldn't do that."

"I wasn't expecting it! I had no preparation! I thought we were going in for a tummyache!" said Evie.

"It was the terrible unexpectedness," said Bert. "So Evie said couldn't we wait."

"And the doctor said, well, we could."

"A little."

"But not too long. Because Quincehead don't have too long," said Evie, and a sob burst out of her. She put her head down and buried her face in Quincehead's fur.

"A few hours," said Bert. "Because his spleen is going to explode otherwise."

"It just didn't seem right, him dying there in a place he don't like to begin with," said Evie.

"He don't like the vet's," said Bert.

"Even though he's always been good at the vet's."

"He never makes a fuss."

"The first time we brought him in, the vet said he was the best-behaved dog he'd ever seen."

"The vet was pretty upset himself, Evie. He teared right up when he said Quincehead would have to be put down."

"I didn't see that."

"You were distraught," said Bert. "You weren't seeing much of anything." And then he ran his hand through his hair, even though he didn't have much hair left. "Anyhow, Primrose, the vet said he'd come at the end of his day and his receptionist called right before you got here and said he's just finishing up now. So it won't be long. You might not want to stay."

"No, it's okay," I said. It never occurred to me to just walk out, although to stay made me feel complicit. It seemed terrible, all of us except Quincehead knowing what was going to happen.

"I just don't want him to be scared," said Evie. "I didn't want him to see me cry or get the idea I'm too upset neither, because that might upset him more. Or make him nervous something bad is going to happen."

But she couldn't stop crying and Quincehead, to be honest, looked too out of it to care. He just lay there, bloated and breathing shallowly.

Evie, without looking up, put one hand on my forearm, then quickly put her hand back on Quincehead. As if she wanted to keep him company as long as possible.

"I think it gives Quincehead some comfort you're here too," said Evie.

"Now he's got his whole family here," said Bert.

Quincehead was breathing less now, more slowly and shallowly as if already the breath was leaving him, the way the waves crash in at high tide and then lessen, becoming quieter and quieter until the sea is still.

"We had no way of knowing he was so ill. His stomach don't look no different from the way it did the time he ate Evie's salade Niçoise with mini marshmallows," said Bert. "Does it, Evie?" But Evie just nodded. She couldn't talk any more; that much was clear. But Bert seemed to need to.

"We couldn't figure out what had happened to it. Evie left it on the counter in the bowl while she hung up clothes on the line."

No one said anything.

"When she got in, it was gone."

I felt like I should say something to keep Bert company but I couldn't think of anything. I was busy watching Evie. And I thought it must be especially hard for her to let Quincehead go anywhere by himself when she had always been there to take care of him.

"That's how we found out Quincehead could climb stepladders," said Bert. "Because that's how he got up on the table to eat the salad."

It was only Bert and pauses now. It gave the time waiting a kind of strange staccato effect. It had the same rhythm as a sports announcer doing a play-by-play.

"He's always been a smart dog. That's why he could figure out that stepladder."

"We've had Quincehead a long time. Fourteen years."

"I think he had a good life."

"But it's not long enough. No dog's life is long enough."

"Not long enough with *us*. It couldn't *be* long enough with us. But it was a good life, Evie."

She nodded.

"He certainly had some good meals."

"He liked the salade Niçoise with mini marshmallows, that's for sure."

"That's how we found out Quincehead liked marshmallows."

"But marshmallows didn't like him."

In the next pause we heard a car pull into the gravel drive of the trailer park.

"I don't know if I can stand it," said Bert, "when it comes down to it. Do you mind if I go to the bedroom now?"

"You go, Bert," said Evie. "There isn't any other place I *could* be."

"You're awful brave, Evie. You always were."

"No, people is different, is all," said Evie. "What we can stand is different. I couldn't stand *not* being here."

Bert didn't say anything else but we watched his slow shuffle into the bedroom. He didn't even turn around to close the door.

"It can be a cruel world for the gentle creatures. Sometimes there ain't nothing you can do. Not even for the things you love best. Not even for the things that trust you to care for them," said Evie.

And then the vet came.

Evie's Salade Niçoise with
Mini Marshmallows

Line a salad bowl with lettuce leaves. Evie is a very relaxed cook and she doesn't stress too much about what kind of lettuce or how much. She says you'll know it when you see it. She takes a can of green beans and sprinkles them about, and some chopped green onion. She slices three tomatoes or so and throws those on. Then she peels and boils three potatoes and slices and adds them after they are cooled. She says if you have time or are serving the salad to people who care about such things, you can arrange it in a pretty manner. Open two cans of tuna and spread that around too. Add four to six chopped hard-boiled eggs. If you have a hard-boiled egg slicer it makes it look very professional. But you don't always want it to. Sometimes homey is a nice look too. Finally, if you are serving it to anchovy people you can add a can of those spread about, but you'd better know if you have anchovy eaters or not. Then a third of a cup of chopped black olives and, if you want to run up quite the grocery bill, some capers. But it's not crucial. Finally, put some vinaigrette on it. Not too much. No one likes a sloppy salad. Right before serving toss a handful or so of mini marshmallows about. The colored ones look the most artistic.

What Happened at Dinner

I DIDN'T GO TO Evie and Bert's for a while after that because I knew they needed breathing room to grieve. It seems sometimes that if you worry about something enough or are upset enough, it should change the outcome. All your worry should be able to be traded in for a good result. I know that's superstitious but somehow I can't help thinking I can save the things I love with the force of my feelings. But none of us had saved Quincehead. And I knew Evie felt this was a great betrayal. That the unspoken promise she had made and believed in was that she would keep him safe forever. That nothing bad would happen to him as long as she was there. But something had.

Now I was a little worried about Bert and Evie because I was no longer living with them and neither was

Quincehead and they had no little creature on whom to exert their generous natures.

I hoped they were doing okay but when I ran into Bert in town he told me that Evie was just flattened with loss and not up to visitors. He looked pretty flattened himself but still he took Mallomar for a walk down the beach with me and smiled as he watched Mallomar chase seagulls and then come to us for praise over and over. After that, Mallomar and I walked Bert back to the trailer park. He invited me in but at that second Mallomar had to pee, so I walked her around the corner of the trailer just as Evie came racing to the door and pulled Bert inside.

"Guess who was on the phone?" she asked. "Come get some freeziolla and I'll tell you."

The door closed behind them. I waited a couple of minutes outside but Bert didn't come out so I guessed he forgot me in whatever excitement was going on, and I started to leave. I was glad that Evie sounded so excited again about something. As I got to the entrance to the trailer park, I heard their door open and Evie yelled from the top step, "Primrose, come in and have some freeziolla! Bert just remembered you were out here!"

"I have to go home!" I called back. "But call me with the recipe! I want it for my notebook!"

She nodded and waved and closed the door. She looked a little better but I knew there would be a gaping hole in her heart for a while. You can't replace one dog with another any more than you can replace one person with another, but that's not to say you shouldn't get more dogs and people in your life. Even though no one you love is replaceable, you need a dog for the dog place in the heart, I decided, and a child for the child place, if you have a child place in your heart, not everyone does, or a dog place, either, I guess. I've known people who have a ferret place, to which I can only say I am thankful I was not born with one of *those*. A best friend is probably only replaced with a best friend, although I wouldn't know because through circumstances beyond my control I have never had one. I wondered dispiritedly if I ever would.

It is a terrible thing to have pockets of emptiness where something or someone should be. I felt it when my parents were missing. Now that I saw them every night, that pocket was filled, but after-school time could be a bit barren. The house was empty in a particularly echoey way after school. My mother used to always be there, except for the year when she was on a deserted island. Since being rescued, my parents had found themselves short of cash. My mom needed a job. Luckily that was when Miss Clarice arrived in Coal Harbor all the way from Duncan, opened her B and B and hired my mom. Jobs in Coal Harbor are hard to come by and my mom probably couldn't have found one if Miss Clarice hadn't opened her B and B. I was happy for her but it meant I came home to an empty house. Miss Clarice told my mother there would be no set hours for her, which at first made my mother feel it would all be relaxed and informal and charming, but it turned out what Miss Clarice meant was that she would pay my mother a set fee, for which she would work her as much as she needed, which turned out to be always. My mother didn't feel she could complain. They both knew there were a lot of people in town who would be more than happy to take her job.

Sometimes after school I got lonely, and then usually I either went to Evie and Bert's or helped Miss Bowzer out at The Girl on the Red Swing. She was teaching me how to cook and I was trying to move the romance along between her and my uncle Jack.

When my parents had returned from being lost at sea it had looked as if a full-scale romance was about to blossom between Miss Bowzer and Uncle Jack but instead they had just drifted along as usual. He, coming in and making remarks about her menu, which he thought she should spruce up for the new element moving into his town houses; and she, studying him with the same detached disdain she reserved for people who didn't quite live up to her standards. I knew she didn't like his line of work. He was a developer in a town that didn't particularly want developing, but other than that he was a fine man. I wanted to tell her she shouldn't be so picky, people's professions don't say *everything* about them. I wanted to tell him that maybe he should shut up about the menu. He was usually the soul of tact but I think he enjoyed tweaking Miss Bowzer and watching her reaction and didn't seem to notice that it wasn't making her like him any better. Nevertheless I could see why he did it. She was really lovely when angry. It made her green eyes flash. It was as if you could see in that flash the storm within her. As if her eyes, like lightning beneath a thunderhead, became the jewel-like advertisement for the power of the storm. I didn't give either of them any helpful behavioral hints, of course. Even I recognize what someone else might think is none of my business. Once in a state of despair at some offhanded insult Uncle Jack had just made, I did mention when I got him alone that if you're courting someone, insulting them is probably not a good place to start. I tried to make this sound like a general observation and nothing I had noticed anyone I was related to doing lately, but he seemed to see through this and looked startled. Then he said, "I'm not courting her. Courtship implies marriage and I'm not the marrying kind, Primrose. And clearly neither is Miss Bowzer. Some folks are and some aren't."

This kind of took the wind out of my sails, and anyhow I disagreed. If anyone was the marrying sort, it seemed to me it was Uncle Jack. And as for Miss Bowzer, she was the type who would never marry just because it was expected but if she did fall in love, would do so head over heels and stay married until the end of time. She once told me she was waiting for the type of marriage my parents had, where my mother had followed my father out into the storm, looking for his boat, forsaking all else. That was true love, she said, and rare as rare could be and the only kind for her. She was looking for someone who could do that, forsake all else. And Uncle Jack might not think he was courting Miss Bowzer, but something in his manner said he was. I think we have all kinds of different parts of ourselves stored away and waiting and sometimes some of them get unleashed on us without us even knowing. I could tell he wasn't being disingenuous or simply lying when he said he wasn't courting her; he really didn't seem to be aware that the courting part of him was unleashed and on the loose. Maybe he thought he flirted with her just the same as he did with everyone. He couldn't help being charming. I thought the flirting he did with her was of a different sort but in case this was just wishful thinking, I asked my mother what she thought.

"Of course he's in love with her," said my mother. "Do you know what they're like, Primrose? They're like those magnets that push each other away when they get closer."

Jack was her half brother and didn't look like her. She has a fox face and he has a pig face but in a nice way. He's tall and blond, broad-shouldered and ruddy. My mother has sandy hair. I have red hair and freckles. None of us look like each other. If you saw us lined up you would never guess we were family. My mother didn't even meet Uncle Jack until she was older. He was a drifter and was always flitting about developing and doing deals and in the military and in general not available to family. But when my mother got herself lost at sea, the town council looked for a relative for me, and by a fluke Jack showed up in Coal Harbor and solved everyone's problem. Ever since, my mother had felt an indebtedness to her brother. Part of this was manifested in a determination to figure out a more stable life for him, and I could see that this conversation had started wheels turning in her brain.

"We should do something to help this along," she said as she bustled about making dinner.

"I wouldn't," said my father, who was seated on the couch with his newspaper. "Jack always seems to me more than capable of paddling his own canoe."

"Well, we can have them both to dinner, can't we? That's just civilized."

"Uh-huh," said my dad, not sounding convinced in the least.

"He's my brother. There's nothing more natural than having him for dinner. It's just that I've been so busy at the B and B. We never *have* had Miss Bowzer for dinner and shame on us for that, the way she lets Primrose hang out in that restaurant."

"I help her!" I protested.

"And was one of the people who watched over her

when we disappeared," my mother went on as if she hadn't heard me. "I suppose we should plan on Sunday when I'm not working."

"But Miss Bowzer works Sunday," I said.

"Oh, of course," said my mother.

"The only night she has off is Monday and she said the other day that she might have to start keeping the restaurant open then too because she barely kept body and soul together this winter."

My mom and dad looked at each other over the top of my head and my mother nodded.

"You know it's hard to survive in a small town on one income," said my mother. "Much better to be married."

"Although she seems to have done okay so far," said my dad, rustling his paper and pulling it up over his face again as if this were his last comment on the topic.

"So far," said my mother, pursing her lips. "Monday it is. I'll just tell Miss Clarice that I must leave early and that is that. Now, let's think of a menu."

"You don't even know yet if they'll come," I said.

"Well, that's your job, Primrose. You invite her. Jack just eats TV dinners every night anyway. Why *wouldn't* he come for supper? We ought to have him more often. TV dinners have no nutrition."

"He likes TV dinners!" I said. "Especially the chicken ones."

"Those chicken TV dinners always remind me of rat pieces. Those stringy little legs in there," said my mother.

"Even if they are, why ruin it for him?" said my father quietly from behind his paper.

My mom didn't bother answering but bustled into the kitchen with a pile of cookbooks and plopped them on the table between us. We had six cookbooks, all from the Fishermen's Aid Society's yearly cookbook sale, the proceeds from which went to help fishermen's families who were suffering for one reason or another. There was never very much money in the fund. Just enough to maybe pay a grocery bill or buy school clothes. I would probably have gotten some of it when my parents disappeared if Uncle Jack hadn't shown up when he did.

As if reading my thoughts, my mother said, "I ought to try to find another fund-raiser for Fishermen's Aid. The cookbook sale is never enough."

"But I'm collecting a whole notebook of new recipes," I protested. "Ones we haven't used yet. Evie even called me with her freeziolla recipe. Well, I suppose I could always turn my recipes into a real cookbook and send it to a real publisher. A fund-raiser for me. How do you get something published?"

"I don't know. I don't think it's that easy," said my mom. "Who is that lady who lives on the edge of town who published a book about cats? She sure made it sound hard. She said being a writer was like being a cross between a ditchdigger and a pit pony."

My dad snorted. "A writer? Wasn't her book just a bunch of photographs of cats?"

"Never mind, I just had another idea. Maybe we'll do a *youth* cookbook this year with Coal Harbor's youths' favorite recipes or something. Let's think about it. A different twist would be good. I bet people are getting tired of the same old thing. Mrs. Cranston entered her shepherd's pie recipe three years in a row and I haven't had the heart to tell her because, frankly, I suspect it's the only thing she knows how to cook."

"Maybe you should write Miss Honeycut," said my father from behind his paper.

"The only thing I ever saw her make was lemon cookies for Uncle Jack. And besides, she doesn't even live here anymore," I said.

"No, about money for the aid society," said my dad.

"Oh, that Miss Honeycut!" said my mother, snorting with derision.

Miss Honeycut was our school guidance counselor when my parents disappeared at sea and had been instrumental in getting me pulled out of my happy situation with Uncle Jack and put into a foster home. This had worked out fine because the foster home had been with Bert and Evie but she hadn't *known* it would work out fine. Miss Honeycut just wanted me out of the way so she could go after Uncle Jack. Her father had owned about all of the North of England and she had inherited it at his death and gone back there. And that had been the end of Miss Honeycut, or so I had thought.

"Besides, Miss Honeycut may be rich but she's cheap," I said.

"Maybe so," said my father. "But she is about to lay a pack of money on Coal Harbor. Listen to this."

He began to read an article. Miss Honeycut apparently had written the mayor that she was to disperse some charitable funds on behalf of her dead father and she wanted to do something for Coal Harbor, where she said she had spent some of her happiest years. This, I'm certain, was news to everyone in Coal Harbor. She always looked like she had a pickle up her nose. She always looked at me as if my being *in particular* was pickle-worthy. But she looked as if quite a lot of other people were a source of great misery too, so I never really took it personally. It *did* make me feel vaguely apologetic whenever I was in her presence. Loneliness surrounded her like a little fog, and you could tell she didn't like it but had been taught not to complain. She was valiantly doing the best with what she had. She surrounded herself with colleagues and she talked about her friends all over the world. And she told endless anecdotes in an effort to be politely entertaining and do the right thing. The problem was she was trying so hard to do the right thing that *she* never really inhabited her life, it seemed to me. It was run by some kind of phantom adjudicator whose standards she never quite lived up to. She held everyone else to this adjudicator's standards as well, so there was no help for any of us. And it didn't seem to matter how many so-called friends she had, she never connected especially with one person, and if you can't connect especially with one person, maybe you can't really connect with anyone. This is the kind of loneliness that existed for her, different from the just-not-knowing-anyone loneliness. And it worried me because I didn't have a best friend and I certainly didn't want to end up like Miss Honeycut, available for deathbed appearances and christenings and not particularly missed in between. I had a bunch of special grown-up friends but that was limited too because they had lives that were complicated in ways different from mine. I couldn't be a party to them. I was more an accessory. Of course there was Eleanor Milkmouse but she was only a friend of convenience. And maybe even desperation, because it was so embarrassing to have no special friend at all. We didn't really understand each other. I feared I was Miss Honeycut in a younger format, the difference being that I really wanted a best friend and was sure, given the opportunity, I could have one, whereas I always had the feeling Miss Honeycut could be presented with someone perfect for her and still somehow never make that connection. It was almost as if loneliness had become her best friend.

The article went on to say that anyone who had a

suggestion for a charitable Coal Harbor cause should write to Miss Honeycut, and gave her manor house address, which, I was interested to note, was Honeycut Hall, without even a street name. Imagine, I thought, your home being so enormous and well known that all you had to say was you lived at Honeycut Hall somewhere in the North of England and all your mail got there fine.

"Excellent," said my mother when my father finished reading. "What is a better or more fitting use for this money than the Fishermen's Aid? How much money is involved, does she say?"

"Half a million pounds," said my father.

There was a stunned silence.

"Is that the same as half a million dollars?" I asked.

"Considerably more," said my father.

"We wouldn't even know what to *do* with so much money," said my mother.

"Well, don't tell *her* that," said my father. "And apparently it's only a small portion of the money she has been assigned to give away."

"After all, she *does* own half of England," I said.

"We'd only need *some* of the money," said my mother. "Just a portion of that would help so many families through a bad winter. Or we could set up a foundation and the interest could help families year after year. We'd never have to have another cookbook drive."

"I like the cookbook drives," I said. "How else are you going to learn how everyone else in town eats?"

"You'd better write soon," said my father to my mom. "I have a feeling there's going to be no end of people pleading their cases."

"I will. Tonight," said my mother, and then we sat down and began flipping through cookbooks.

But I wasn't really paying attention. I couldn't get out of my head the idea that Miss Honeycut's best years had been spent here, where she had seemed so lonely and out of place. Where had her worst years been, and what was it like for her now in England in her manor house with all that money? Shouldn't *these* be the best years of her life? Owning half of England? But maybe the reason she was cheap was that money hadn't ever made her that happy and she didn't expect it to make other people happy either.

"Chicken?" my mom asked me for the second time, and I tried to pull my thoughts back to the here and now. "*Real* chicken as opposed to pieces of rat?"

"I don't know. Seems a little dull," I said. "Unless you want to make cornflake chicken. We haven't made that in a while."

"Ummm," said my mother, biting her lip and flipping pages.

"Yeah," I said, thinking about it. "Let's make cornflake chicken and mashed potatoes and ersatz gravy and peas and biscuits! Let's do a Southern dinner. Uncle Jack would like that and I bet Miss Bowzer would too."

Ersatz gravy was one of my mother's inventions. It

was supposed to be healthy gravy because it used corn-starch, not fat, as a thickener but it turned out to taste really good too.

"Ummm," said my mother, still flipping. "Maybe we can find something a little fancier."

"Fancier?" I said. "That's a Sunday-type supper."

"Oh, I don't think so," my mother said, looking uncomfortable.

"What's wrong with it?" I pressed. "You think it's fancy when *we* have it."

"It's fine for Jack. I just don't want to serve a professional chef something made with *cornflakes*, okay? And ersatz gravy is definitely not for company."

"You don't have to impress Miss Bowzer. I've already told her about the ersatz gravy and she said she'd like to try it sometime."

"Well, Miss Bowzer's very polite. And I know she serves honest, unpretentious food. Except for that silly thing with the lentils Jack made her put on the menu. But I'd still like to at least look like I know better, especially as Miss Bowzer has never eaten here before. I don't want her to think we eat things like cornflake chicken and ersatz gravy all the time."

"But we do."

"Well, she doesn't have to know that, okay? Or think that even if we eat that way we don't know better than to cook such things for guests."

"And Uncle Jack didn't *make* her put it on the menu. He suggested it. You can't *make* Miss Bowzer do anything. She did it to reward him because she thought he'd done a fine thing, saving lives in that fire."

"What about steak?"

"Steak doesn't take any cooking skills. It's like saying, I couldn't be bothered. I mean, if you're going to make steak for company, you might as well go all the way and just meet them in a field and chew on a raw cow."

"I know what!" said my mother, stabbing a cookbook page with her finger and looking elated. "Lamb!"

• • •

We found lamb chops in the bottom of the freezer at the general store. They were expensive and slightly freezer burned and Mr. Barrista warned my mom that they'd been sitting there for a long time but it didn't seem to matter to her, it was elegance ho. Besides, she said, the cost would just get lost in the general bill at the end of the month and she would economize somewhere else.

For the next week I was very excited about the dinner even if I wasn't mad for the menu, except for the ersatz gravy, which my mother had agreed to make as a compromise because let's face it, serving grilled lamb is basically like serving grilled steak and requires no feats of imagination.

Both Miss Bowzer and Uncle Jack had accepted the invitation immediately, which I took as a good sign. But when they got to our door they looked startled to see each other and then I realized I hadn't told each the other was coming. I hadn't done this on purpose but I might have unconsciously.

"Ah, Miss Bowzer," said Uncle Jack, looking very pleased after the initial surprise.

"Oh," said Miss Bowzer. And then she clearly couldn't think of anything else to say and blushed right down her neck.

I showed them in and we sat down on the couch. My dad, who had just gotten in minutes before, washed the worst of the fishy smell off his hands with lemon and then joined us.

I was wearing my nicest sweater. Miss Bowzer wore a polka-dot dress and *lipstick* and looked uncomfortable without an apron on. She kept wiping her hands on her dress, realizing it wasn't an apron and probably that her hands weren't dirty, and then cracking her knuckles. It was not the most attractive mating display. My father kept pouring Uncle Jack scotches and giving him sympathetic looks. My mother was way perkier and more cheerful than usual. So much so that she bordered on the manic. But she hadn't been able to get out of work as early as she had demanded and had had to run home and throw dinner together and now even though she was caught up and had things cooking, she couldn't seem to slow down again. When Miss Bowzer saw that my mom was wearing blue jeans and no makeup she looked even more uncomfortable and overdressed. I wanted to pull her aside and tell her my mom simply hadn't had time to glam up, even though the truth is my mom never wears makeup or fancy clothes. I thought Miss Bowzer looked really nice and someone should mention it but it was as if we'd all taken an unspoken vow not to mention *the dress*. This, of course, made it much worse because under normal relaxed circumstances someone would have complimented her on her good grooming. You ought to appreciate the effort, any effort people make.

Uncle Jack alone retained his savoir faire as if he were completely at home with people who would really be better off heavily sedated. He kept everyone entertained with tales of developing land down island. And every time Miss Bowzer started to look especially uncomfortable and out of place, he leaped in and engaged her in questions or asked for her opinion on some business venture. Miss Bowzer was always happiest when offering an opinion. She was one of those people who knew exactly what she thought about any subject you'd care to proffer. So it was a comforting activity for her and for a while after, she'd look relaxed again. Miss Bowzer didn't seem to mind Uncle Jack's development adventures as long as the development was happening someplace else. Although I thought we might be in trouble when she said, "Just tell me who but a total skunk would want a lot of strangers coming in and gunking up the waters and chopping down the trees and clogging the roads and putting up artificial light at night when it's no business being anything but dark, and turning the west coast of Vancouver Island into a concrete mess like Florida?"

"You forgot annihilating the wildlife, including those skunks you mentioned," said Uncle Jack.

And then Miss Bowzer remembered her manners and that she was in our house and not her restaurant and toned it down, even laughed at several of his escapades. Uncle Jack had been busy developing Coal Harbor by building seaside town houses during the period when my parents were lost at sea, but after they were rescued and he didn't have to worry about me, he turned his attention to more lucrative ventures down island. The town houses he had built by Coal Harbor's docks had been called a lot of nasty things by people in town, including a carbuncle on Coal Harbor's nose, which was maybe overdoing things a bit. People did get worked up when it looked like we were going to lose what we all held so dear, namely the perfection of Coal Harbor just as it was. There are so few places that are perfect just as they are. But Uncle Jack, maybe because it's the nature of a developer, felt every thing and every place could be improved upon and it was figuring out how and then doing it that excited him. Also seeing how much money he could make. I don't think he wanted the money per se, he just wanted to see *if* he could make it. He had made and lost fortunes many times in his life and it didn't seem to dim one iota his enthusiasm for the romance of business.

I forgot that Uncle Jack was a lefty and sat him next to Miss Bowzer, where his cutting arm kept knocking into hers, which might have been a good thing if she'd been the sly, flirty, go-ahead-and-knock-into-me-with-your-knife-arm-you-big-lug type. But she wasn't. She was more the I'm-going-to-try-to-ignore-the-line-of-bruises-forming-up-my-arm type. If I was less invested in their future happiness I might have found it entertaining. Well, all right, it was entertaining anyway.

"And *now*," said Uncle Jack, continuing his anecdote as he picked hopelessly at the teeny bit of meat left on his chop. Out of deference to Miss Bowzer, I guess, he wasn't picking up the bone and gnawing on it. But he wouldn't leave it half-eaten either and kept trying to get at the tiny stringy bit of lamb with his knife and fork, which sometimes slipped against the greasy chop and made terrible clattering noises on the plate. I saw a splatter of ersatz gravy land perilously close to Miss Bowzer's polka-dotted dress. And of course it all resulted in yet more jabs to her arm with his elbow, all for the sake of good manners. I wanted to scream, FOR HEAVEN'S SAKE, THERE'S MORE IN THE KITCHEN. Although there wasn't more lamb. It was expensive enough giving everyone three chops. But there was a swell dessert—floating island. I had chosen it and helped to make it myself. My mother had wanted to go with chocolate cake but we had never made floating island and I had always wanted to and it's not the type of thing you make just for yourselves. "You ought to make something fancy so she won't think all you know is ersatz gravy," I said to my mother, and that, of course, sealed the deal.

I pointed out the ersatz gravy to Miss Bowzer and reminded her that she had said she wanted to try it and she said, "Ah, um, yes," but she didn't seem to really be paying attention. I noticed she had poured it on her potatoes and eaten it but my sense of things was that she hadn't tasted it at all. She was still too busy being nervous and overdressed.

"Anyhow," Uncle Jack wrapped up his last hilarious anecdote about development by Campbell River, "I'm done with that project."

Miss Bowzer didn't respond. Just sat there in her polka-dotted dress, looking uncomfortable, her chops half finished.

"So, Jack," said my father. "What's next?"

"There's always something next with this guy!" said my mother, through a mouthful of mashed potatoes and peas, while gesticulating wildly with her knife and fork.

"Well, Miss Bowzer may have some suspicions," said Uncle Jack.

This had the effect of making Miss Bowzer suddenly

look suspicious. It was actually a rather attractive look for her. It made her appear all fiery and romantic. Angry and suspicious were good looks for her and I thought this was lucky as those were the two emotions Uncle Jack seemed to inspire in her the most.

"Why should I know anything about what you're doing next?" she demanded.

"Because it's already started right across the street from you," said Uncle Jack. "I thought by now you might have gotten normally curious and gone and at least looked in the window."

"Jack," said my mother, tittering in a fake way. "I'm sure we're all normal around here."

Why couldn't everyone just be *themselves*? I really felt frustrated by not being able to choreograph everyone's behavior. I liked everyone at that table and I couldn't believe how wrong they were all getting it. I felt I should hand out scripts.

"Are you *saying* I'm not normal?" Miss Bowzer asked, turning with steely eyes to Uncle Jack. Before he could answer, my father interrupted.

"Were you the one that bought that building across from The Girl on the Red Swing? The one where there's construction going on?" Heretofore my dad had been preoccupied by figuring out exactly how much meat he could get off his chops. He was the only one who picked them up and gnawed. He'd study them as if he couldn't believe there wasn't something he was missing. Not at ten dollars a pound. Then he'd pick them up and go at them again. It seemed like an engrossing activity, practically a new hobby, so that only now was he waking up to the table conversation.

"I'm the one," said Uncle Jack proudly through a mouthful of potatoes and ersatz gravy. "New enterprise."

"Wow. That place has been empty for as long as I can remember. I'm surprised it's still standing. People have been talking for years about tearing it down before it *falls* down. Wasn't it an old hotel back in the day?"

"Yep, and it's not in such bad shape. The timbers are sound. I was getting tired of always traveling around down island on business. I thought it would be nice to open up something closer to home so I'd *be* home."

Normally Uncle Jack loved to roam. My mother used to call him old hotfoot Jack. She threw him a piercing look and then turned to Miss Bowzer.

"My, my! Then I guess you and Jack will be *neighbors!*" She said this with so much enthusiasm it was as if the concept of neighbors had just been invented. By her. "Isn't that nice? Well, this is a surprise. Jack is always such a *dark horse*. We never know what to expect from him from one moment to the next. He's just FULL of surprises." She shrieked this last, which made even my unflappable father look at her in alarm. But she was oblivious and looked around, pretending to be speaking to the table in general, but really she might as well have had a megaphone pointed at Miss Bowzer's ear, calling out, "Eligible bachelor. Tons of fun. Catch him while you can!"

My father picked up another already-gnawed chop and yawned. I wanted to pass my mother her better script because I wasn't so sure that *general unexpectedness* was what Miss Bowzer was looking for in a mate.

"So tell us, Jack," my mother went on with manic beaming approval, "what is it that you're opening?"

"A restaurant," said Jack.

And then I knew the evening was over.

Freeziolla

Put an undrained ten-ounce package of defrosted frozen strawberries in a bowl with a can of drained crushed pineapple. Add one cup of strawberry yogurt, one quarter cup of powdered sugar and one half cup of mini marshmallows. Line an ice cube tray with foil extending a few inches over both sides. Pour the mixture in and fold the extra foil over the top. Freeze it for three hours, until solid. Lift it out of the tray. Let it stand a bit to soften so that you can cut it in triangles. (Evie says triangles look the prettiest.) Arrange each piece on a lettuce leaf and put a pineapple ring on top to garnish. You can tell people this is a salad. People in certain moods will believe anything.

Ersatz Gravy

Take a can of consommé and heat it with some poultry seasoning. About two tablespoons or so. Bring it to a boil and add a tablespoon or so of cornstarch which you have mixed with a quarter cup of water. Mix that in and let it cook a bit to thicken the gravy. That's it. If people know how it's made they will pretend not to like it but they really will.

Floating Island

Beat eight egg whites, three quarters of a cup of sugar and a pinch of salt until you get a meringue. Boil water and let simmer and into it drop four large glops of the meringue. These will be the islands. Poach them in the water for two minutes on one side and four on the other and then drain them on paper towels.

Take four egg yolks and beat with a pinch of salt and one quarter cup of sugar. Scald two cups of milk and add it to the egg yolks, beating frantically so the eggs don't cook. Place the custard in a double boiler and stir constantly until it thickens. Remove from heat and cool a bit and then add a teaspoon of vanilla and a teaspoon of lemon rind grated very, very tiny. Chill this.

Finally, to assemble, put the sea of custard into four dessert bowls and float a meringue island in each one.

If your parents have been stranded on an island for a year, this is a very poignant dessert. And even if they haven't, it's pretty good.

What Happened to Miss Bowzer When She Was Young

"A RESTAURANT? ARE YOU crazy?" said Miss Bowzer, no longer able to retain her polite demeanor, polka-dotted dress or no.

"Are you upset? Why are you upset?" asked Uncle Jack, putting down his knife and fork and looking stunned. "I'm doing high end. You're doing low end. Different markets altogether."

"LOW end?" squawked Miss Bowzer.

"I don't mean that in a bad way. I just mean cheap, well, more *affordable* meals."

"*Cheap* food?" said Miss Bowzer.

It amazed me that Uncle Jack, who was the most clever and tactful person I knew, seemed to lose all these skills the second he came in contact with Miss Bowzer. It never failed.

My mother got the floating islands on the table very quickly after that. The one she slung on the table in front of my father practically skidded into his lap. You would think that would take everyone's mind off of things—the anticipation of custard on his pants—but Miss Bowzer, who had been turning what looked to me a dangerous shade of red, didn't seem to notice and excused herself to go to the bathroom. When she returned it was as if she had Krazy Glued her lips together in there, because she hardly said a word the rest of the night. Ten minutes after her last sip of coffee she thanked my mother for her fine meal and hospitality and left.

I was deflated. You know exactly how bad a time someone has had by how soon after dinner they leave and how formal they are about it. Jack stayed on long enough to help us clear the table and wash the dishes. He and my parents talked about other things and never mentioned the restaurant once. I think my mother was afraid that if she did, she would hit him over the head with whatever pan was handiest. When he finally left I went up to bed. As I climbed the stairs I heard my father's voice below saying cheerily, "Well, that was a pleasant evening."

• • •

I didn't see much of Miss Bowzer after that. I was a little embarrassed that it was my family that had upset her with its version of *The Dating Game*. I knew Uncle Jack hadn't intended his restaurant announcement to mean and-by-the-way-I'm-putting-you-out-of-business-pass-the-salt, but that's what it must have sounded like to her.

I didn't see Uncle Jack much after that, either, because he was very busy getting his restaurant built.

"She'll see," he explained to me one day when I ran into him on the street. "She's an excellent chef but she doesn't understand the first thing about business. My business will be, if anything, *good* for her business."

I didn't see how this would be so. I followed him back to his restaurant on the pretext of helping him carry his purchases but really so that he could explain his reasoning to me. Then I, in turn, could explain it to Miss Bowzer.

"Listen, people get tired of the same old thing. They'll come to my restaurant for special occasions and Miss Bowzer's for everyday fare. Choice just makes eating out all the more enticing. There was a study, Primrose, that said people eat more when they have more choices. If it's just two things in the fridge they won't eat so much. If there's twenty things, they'll graze from taste to taste. We're just giving people more choices, which will inspire more grazing."

"But she has a lot of stuff on her menu already. People already *have* choices," I argued. Then a chunk of ceiling fell right in front of us and Uncle Jack moved me over a few feet and started up the stairs to see "what the heck they were doing up there."

"Maybe you'd better go, Primrose," he called down, sounding all distracted, so I left.

If this was the way they were going to court, each waiting for the other to make a move, both being proud and independent, they would never connect. I couldn't arrange another dinner. That would be too obvious, but there must be some way I could help them along.

I took a bike ride out Jackson Road. Jackson Road is a good thinking road. There is nothing but treed mountains until you come to Miss Clarice's farm and B and B. There is a stillness there you don't find other places. It's the *quality* of the stillness. It's like the stillness is thicker and there's more in it, the way ersatz gravy is just consommé until the cornstarch goes in and then it has what chefs call viscosity. When I am there I can feel my thoughts expand until they feel full of viscosity themselves, so that before I'd even ridden the length of the road, I had a plan.

I biked furiously back to the library and got out a Julia Child cookbook. My mother had some tapes of Julia Child's old cooking shows and I knew she was considered a gourmet. I ran my finger down the table of contents until I had what I needed and then I headed back to The Girl on the Red Swing.

I came in through the alley kitchen door.

It seemed to me that Miss Bowzer, who is a furious chopper anyway, was chopping with special ferocity.

"I was just visiting Uncle Jack."

"Feh," said Miss Bowzer, and chopped even harder.

"His ceiling doesn't want to stay up," I said casually, pulling over a stool and chewing on a piece of celery.

"Ha!" said Miss Bowzer.

Apparently this was going to be a day of one-syllable responses.

"He was saying that he'd probably hire a gourmet chef to run his restaurant. Someone who could cook the kind of things you can't. You know, really hard recipes. Like *boeuf bourguignon*."

Miss Bowzer stopped chopping. She whirled around.

"He told you I couldn't make *boeuf bourguignon*?"

She was spluttering. This was excellent.

"Well, he implied it. Or I inferred it. I can never remember the difference," I said, looking out the window as if the whole thing didn't concern me in the least. In fact, I do know the difference between *inferred* and *implied* because one of the wonderful things about Miss Connon is that she demands people be precise with their language.

"Oh, really? Well, where does he think I went to cooking school?"

"I don't think he thinks you did. I think he thinks you just, you know, picked it up."

"PICKED IT *UP*?" Miss Bowzer's eyes were afire and her neck was getting blotches of red. Maybe I'd gone too far.

"You know, like, on the street."

"ON THE STREET? I'll have him know I went to the Cordon Bleu in Paris for an entire semester!"

"You did?" I said. I hadn't known this. I was impressed.

"*Boeuf bourguignon!* He probably doesn't even know how to spell it."

"Oh, I'm sure you're right. He's probably never even tasted it. He probably wouldn't know a *boeuf bourguignon* if he fell into a pot of it."

"Feh! Hand me that Dutch oven on the shelf behind you."

I handed it to her. "Are you making one now?" I asked.

"*Boeuf bourguignon.* I'll show him!"

"Should I invite him here for dinner?" I asked.

"Feh," she spluttered.

"I mean as a paying customer."

"Huh!"

We were back to one syllable.

"Well, I guess I'll head over there."

"Don't bother!" she said, going to the freezer and getting out some beef. "*I'll* bring it over for him to taste when it's done. The nerve!"

"Well, do you want some help?" I asked.

"No," said Miss Bowzer. "Some things I have to do myself, Primrose. Now skedaddle."

I wondered if I should have mentioned that he's really shy and out of practice when it comes to women. Or would that have been too obvious?

Later, after my own supper, I went over to Uncle Jack's to see what the upshot of the *boeuf bourguignon* episode had been. I was hoping that Miss Bowzer had brought it over and they'd ended up having a romantic candlelit dinner for two. But then who would have minded The Girl on the Red Swing? No, no! That would have been even *better,* if *she'd forgotten her restaurant in the passion of the moment.* Even Uncle Jack would have seen that was a *sign!*

Uncle Jack had papers spread over his kitchen table and there were empty TV dinner trays on the counter. He either hadn't had the *boeuf bourguignon* or she'd only given him a taste. I'm sure if he'd had a whole dinner of it, it would have been filling enough without hauling out the rat chicken.

"Primrose!" he said. "Two visits in one day."

"Oh, here." I handed him some of my mom's cookies. They were the excuse I had come up with for popping in.

"Thanks, I was just wishing I had some dessert. Put them on the counter. I'm sorry but I'm kind of busy."

"I just thought since you probably were eating TV dinners, nothing special, like nothing gourmet, you'd like some homemade dessert. The TV dinners were your first dinner tonight, right?"

"First dinner? What are you talking about?" He looked up from his papers. He was sharp, which was a major stumbling block to my plans, and his eyes scanned my face, but I was getting wise in the ways of the matchmaker and I just stared back at him innocently. I can make my pupils dilate. I used to do this in school when I got bored. You just blur your vision. You can actually feel them dilating. It makes you look innocent and doe-eyed.

Uncle Jack's eyes remained suspiciously on me for a bit and then he said, "Right. Well, I've got to work."

"Okay. For some reason you just smelled kind of like beef when I came in," I said.

He dropped his pen. "You don't say. I don't smell it myself but to assuage your curiosity, I will confess I did have a taste of *boeuf bourguignon*. I'm afraid Miss Bowzer is losing her mind. She came charging over as I was about to leave my restaurant, holding a big casserole dish, piping hot, and yelled at me. 'Just taste this! *Taste* this, you fool!'"

"What did you do?" I asked breathlessly.

"I tasted it. It was good but I see no reason to get hysterical because you have a pot of it."

"Did you *tell* her it was good?"

"I didn't get a chance. I said, 'Is this beef stew?' and she yelled, 'STEW? It's *boeuf bourguignon*, what do you think of *that*!' like that was supposed to have some kind of significance for me."

"So what did you say then?" I asked, gripping the chair in the excitement of the moment.

"I said, 'Ah.'"

"Ah? Jeez, you could have done better than *that*, couldn't you? And what did *she* say?"

"She said, 'HA!'"

What Happened to Miss Bowzer When She Was Young • 45

"Jeez!" I groaned again before I could stop myself.

"What should I make of such a thing?"

"Never mind. After the ha and ah, *THEN* did you tell her it was good?"

"No, because she said, 'Well then! Well then! We'll hear no more about THAT!' and went charging back to her restaurant. I'm telling you, I think she's cracking up. Running a whole restaurant by yourself must be quite a strain. We must get her some help."

"Yeah, yeah. You could have *told* her it was good! Did you ever think of that? If it *was*. *Was* it good?"

Uncle Jack stopped as if to consider. Then he said, "You know, it *was* good. Very tasty, in fact. But I don't know why she had to come charging over with some. She's gotten very defensive since I said that thing about her restaurant."

"Really?" I said coldly. "How odd."

"Odd is the word for it. What do you make of the whole business? *The strange affair of the* boeuf bourguignon, as it shall be hereafter known," he said, and his eyes twinkled for a second and he looked like his old self and not so fraught with worry and paperwork.

"I don't know," I said slowly, my gaze dropping to the floor as if I had to think hard about this. "I know she really values your opinion . . . maybe she needed to make sure the *boeuf* was seasoned right. Or maybe she was hoping you'd taste it and come have dinner at her restaurant with her. It sounds, you know, like she cooked it *just for you*." I thought I might have pushed it too far but Uncle Jack picked up his pen and went back to his papers with a distracted air.

"Yeah, I doubt it," he said. "Now I really have to settle these plans. I don't want to be rude but . . ."

"Okay, I'm going. But not all *bourguignons* are about the *boeuf*!" And with that one little clue, I swept out.

• • •

None of my adult friends seemed available at the moment, being in mourning or consumed with business ventures and a stalled *affaire de coeur* that manifested itself in fine French cuisine, so I was left with Eleanor Milkmouse, whom I hung out with when there was absolutely nothing else to do. Eleanor was kind of lumpy and shapeless, with black straight hair that partially obscured her face. You wanted to reach up and brush it out of the way for her, especially since some of it always seemed to be stuck to her chapped lips or damp forehead or something indeterminate that had dried on her cheek and was best not pondered. She had a nasal condition, which I know wasn't her fault, but somehow I couldn't help feeling she could dry up her nose *occasionally* if she really tried. I once spent ten minutes entertaining the idea of sticking a hair dryer up it. But of course it wouldn't fit. And she didn't seem that keen when I mentioned it. There were always partially used Kleenexes hanging from all her pockets. I don't think she liked me any more than I liked her but she sometimes asked me over for sleepovers and I could never think of an excuse to say no. One day she confessed listlessly that I was her best friend. At first this filled me with horror, that I actually meant something to her; then I realized being appointed her best friend didn't bespeak affection but lack of any other option and I relaxed.

There were only a dozen twelve-year-old girls in Coal Harbor and everyone had paired up in kindergarten except for us. We were left with each other or nobody. Out of pride we put on a show of being friends by choice, and when people had to pick a partner in class at least we had one. The teacher never had to lead us by the wrist to each other and join our sweaty palms together. It was really the most dignified option. Eleanor told me once she thought I was strange because I *"thought about things."* And she kept away from me that whole year my parents had gone missing, as if the condition were contagious. Now that I was hanging out with Eleanor again, I kept thinking maybe we'd find some new common ground. That she couldn't be as boring as she appeared, she must have unplumbed depths. And she probably did, but it didn't make me compatible with what was down there. A lot of what was down there was her undying and undeclared love for Spinky Caldwater. She could rattle on endlessly about him and I found it embarrassing but of course I had to be polite. I wouldn't have minded if I had something similarly boring to rattle on about on a daily basis; then I could have just sat there patiently waiting for my turn. I wanted to think I would find something to make me really like Eleanor but maybe it's better to admit that some people you'll never like and that's that. I couldn't decide whether being with her was worse than being alone. Although, being with her was in many ways *just* like being alone. I ached for a best friend whom I actually liked and respected. For one thing, it was difficult to find stuff both Eleanor and I liked to do. She wanted to play paper dolls and I tried to teach her to cook but she was afraid of making mistakes and her mother wouldn't let her use knives.

"You're twelve!" I said when she confessed to this. "How do you cut your meat?"

"I can use *steak* knives at the table," she said, rolling her eyes. "I can't just, like, you know, chop."

"Well, why don't you tell your mother you think you are ready to chop? Maybe she's waiting for you to make the first move."

As usual Eleanor had no answer. She never argued. She just got quiet. Complete silence was always her last word on everything.

One day after school we were hanging out at her house. I was trying to think of as many positive things as I could about Eleanor. This was slow going but I had finally come up with the fact that she had hardly snorted at all that afternoon when we started making cootie catchers and couldn't find scissors except for kitchen shears and she said she wasn't allowed to use those either because the tips weren't rounded.

"I have to go," I said, and walked right out the door.

I need someone I can talk to, I thought, my feet beating desperately down the pavement toward town. I need someone who can use sharp scissors. I was racing past The Girl on the Red Swing and on impulse burst through the kitchen door.

Miss Bowzer was chopping potatoes with a sharp knife and looking the embodiment of a sane universe.

"I'm never going to have a good friend," I said, telling her the knife and shears story.

"Sure you are, kid," she said, not looking at me. We were both still a little embarrassed about the dinner party and I was embarrassed at the failure of my *boeuf bourguignon* plans. "Next time just pick someone who doesn't blow her nose on my napkins."

"Or doesn't pronounce the *t* in *often*," I added.

"Oh yeah, that makes me crazy too," said Miss Bowzer, lighting a cigarette and puffing the smoke at the ceiling.

I felt better already.

"Anyhow, I get it," said Miss Bowzer contemplatively. "When I was a teenager I thought I was never going to have a boyfriend. All my friends had boyfriends but me. I thought it meant I was ugly or had a rotten personality or something. Or there was something wrong with my femaleness. Like maybe the other girls had natural female wiles I lacked and everyone knew it. Then I ended up with the most sought-after guy in town."

"Is it anyone I know?" I couldn't imagine Miss Bowzer with anyone but Uncle Jack.

"Oh, he's long gone now. I don't know what he's doing. His family moved down to Duncan when he turned seventeen. So he didn't even graduate with us. His name was Dan Sneild."

"That sounds like a made-up villain's name."

"Yes," she said, stopping her chopping, stubbing out her cigarette and pondering it. "He looked like a villain too. That was probably a lot of his appeal. He drove around town on a motorcycle, revving the engine. It was like a mating call. It brought girls out to the street. But he wasn't looking for them, he was looking for me."

She gazed back through time with a satisfied glow.

"You're so beautiful! You must have been *really* beautiful back then," I exclaimed without thinking and then realized how it sounded and my face got warm. But Miss Bowzer didn't mind. She looked at my pink cheeks and laughed and suddenly it was all right between us again.

"Anyhow, he made an excellent first boyfriend. He was romantic in the way girls are romantic, which back then I figured was what romance was supposed to be. He used to buy me used books of poetry and any flowers he could get at the general store. He had a job weekends at the cannery, where his dad was a supervisor. But he never smelled like fish. And he was the only boy in town who didn't smell like Hai Karate. He smelled like the sea." She smiled again. "Not fish. The sea, you know?"

I nodded. My dad comes home at night smelling like salt and the wind. "What was Hai Karate?"

"Oh, a kind of aftershave favored by sixteen-year-old boys when I was growing up. School dances were nearly unbearable because of it. We'd ride all over the back roads in springtime on that motorcycle. We used to go into the B and B your mom works at. It was empty and abandoned then. Just a big old abandoned wilderness farm and we'd sit on the front porch and pretend all we surveyed was ours: the B and B, all the surrounding hills and mountains, all the quiet. I thought, Wouldn't it be something to be part of that great stillness? Like no matter how busy I got, I would be surrounded by and protected by and inside of it and it would be in me too then so I would always have it. Dan didn't get that part when I rattled on about it but he said it would be cool to own some cows. He used to say he was going to make a lot of money and come back and buy it for us someday and we'd talk about the rooms and what would be where and I used to decorate it in my head. I didn't see how we'd have space to run a B and B, what with all the children we'd be having.

I planned on twelve. Ha!" she barked, and for a moment looked sad. "My mother had decorating magazines and I'd pore over them. I loved the idea of it so much, I really thought it would happen. I had every room decorated in my mind. I could tell you in detail how they looked. Sometimes at night when I can't sleep I lie in bed and go over them, detail by detail. But anyhow, now Miss Clarice owns it and that's that," she finished abruptly, and wiped her hands on her apron briskly as if wiping off such nonsense and went back to cutting up potatoes.

We chopped companionably for a bit and then she said, "Anyhow, that's water under the bridge. The point I was trying to make was that everyone makes a friend eventually, Primrose."

But like most good conversations we had strayed so far from the original point that trying to return to it was superfluous.

"Maybe," I said noncommittally.

"Just wait, friends come from unlikely places. Just when you think you're alone, one shows up."

I nodded. "Oh, by the way, Uncle Jack said the *boeuf bourguignon* was tasty but probably a one-dish wonder. That the real test would be how you did a *croque monsieur*." This was the only other French recipe I could think of off the top of my head.

Miss Bowzer dropped her dreamy look and slammed her knife down sideways on the cutting board. "*CROQUE*

MONSIEUR? He doesn't think I can handle a *croque monsieur*? Doesn't he know that's a grilled cheese sandwich? No, of course he doesn't know. And he thinks he can open a high-end restaurant to rival me?"

"I don't think he wants to be your rival—" I began.

"Where is he? Where is he right now?"

"I don't know," I said, sliding off my stool and making for the door. "Probably across the street working on his restaurant."

"You go over there right now and tell him supper is on the way."

I ran happily across the street. Inside his new place, Uncle Jack was covered in plaster dust as usual.

"Miss Bowzer is making you a *croque monsieur* for dinner and bringing it over," I said.

"What? I just had lunch two hours ago. Why is she making me a, what did you call it?"

"*Croque monsieur*. It's a grilled cheese sandwich. I think it's awfully nice of her, busy as she is."

"Well, of course it's *nice*," said Uncle Jack. "I just don't understand why she's suddenly . . ."

But I was out the door before he could finish that thought. Let him ask her himself.

I went home and was lying on my bed, listening to the ticking of the clock in the empty house, staring at the ceiling and wishing one of my parents would come back, when the phone rang. It was Evie.

"Primrose, I have the best surprise for you. Remember we said we had a surprise but it kind of got forgotten what with . . ."

"Yes," I said. I was happy to hear some life in Evie again.

"Well, the surprise comes tomorrow. At least it's supposed to. Can you come over after school and then go to dinner at The Girl on the Red Swing with us?"

"That would be GREAT," I said. I was going to tell her about how I could no longer take another afternoon of Eleanor or the echoing emptiness of our house after school. But she rattled on excitedly and I could tell she wasn't paying attention to my end of the conversation.

"*Guess* who is—"

"EVIE!" I heard Bert say in the background. "You're gonna give it away."

"You're right, Bert. Never mind," said Evie, and hung up.

Croque Monsieur

I had to decide between a recipe for *boeuf bourguignon* and *croque monsieur* but frankly, I think a lot of people in Coal Harbor, if faced with a *boeuf bourguignon* recipe, and all the time and fussing it takes, are going to abbreviate it and take liberties until it becomes beef stew. There is nothing wrong with beef stew but you shouldn't really pretend it is anything else. I therefore leave the *boeuf bourguignons* to people like Miss Bowzer who have been to France and know what's what.

Miss Bowzer says a *croque monsieur* is really a direct order because *croquer* means "to crunch." I think Miss Bowzer likes the French and their predilection for giving orders, even slipping them sneakily into the names of dishes. Miss Bowzer would like to give orders this way too.

Put two tablespoons of butter in a saucepan and melt it. Add three tablespoons of flour and stir for a couple of minutes. Slowly add two cups of hot milk so you get a thick sauce. Take it off the stove and melt some grated Gruyère cheese in there. Maybe about a cup. Add a sprinkle of nutmeg and a chopped basil leaf if you like and some salt and pepper to taste. Toast a dozen pieces of bread. Spread some Dijon mustard on each piece and then put a piece of cheese on half the slices (again, Gruyère, if you can get it, but if you are living someplace really small and the cheese selection is also small—small population,

small cheese selection, as we say in Coal Harbor—
then use Swiss). Put a piece of ham on half the slices.
Then cover with the other piece of toast. Now you
should have six complete ham and cheese sandwiches. Put them in a baking dish and pour the cheese
sauce over all and bake the sandwiches at 400 de-
grees for about ten minutes. Then broil briefly. Serve.
Then *Croque, Monsieur, Croque!!*

What Happened at
The Girl on the Red Swing

I WAS VERY EXCITED the next day and couldn't wait for school to let out. I wondered if the surprise was a new dog, although it seemed a little *soon*. I had to go home and walk Mallomar and feed and water her and do homework and I threw together a casserole and put it in the oven for my mom as a surprise. Miss Clarice gives my mother all the jobs that involve heavy grunt work and she gets home pretty tired. Then finally, done with everything, I more or less ran all the way to Bert and Evie's.

I knocked on their door and as it opened I instinctively looked down, searching for a cockapoo. Instead I saw a pair of enormous tennis shoes. When my eyes traveled back up I found they belonged to a huge teenage boy. Bert and Evie'd gotten a new foster child! I was so pleased for them. I knew they had worried they wouldn't be given any, living all the way out in the sticks.

He was about twice as tall as Bert and Evie and had a strange face. It was too flat and his eyes were a bit too wide apart and the bridge of his nose, like the planes of his face, was a little too flat. It gave him the look of someone who had been hit head-on by a frying pan. He also looked like he was about to cry and at first I thought I'd come at a bad time, but later, when he kept looking exactly the same, I realized it was just the configuration of his features. I thought this was unfortunate for him until I realized it might work in his favor among people who are quick to pity. I wondered if a kindly universe had taken this into consideration upon his birth and declared, He will have a childhood that sucks, but he will be given a face that inspires pity even among foster parents not given to feeling it often. By now I knew that I had lucked out, having Bert and Evie as foster parents. That not all foster parents were kind and generous. Sometimes people took kids in for the money the government gave them for doing so and the kids suffered for it, being the unwanted houseguests attached to the monthly check. Bert and Evie had explained this to me and that they had to be especially careful and sensitive when they took someone in because some kids had not only had a harrowing home life with their real families but subsequently with foster families and had become like feral dogs that feel they must be wary and protective of their space at all times. It made Bert and Evie twice as nurturing. Although Evie had told me once that "you don't want to burden a kid with this, neither. Because not all of them can handle more than they got served up on their plate already. You just got to keep your expansive feelings in check and see what you can do for them that don't require them having to respond more than they want. And sometimes you don't get them but for a few weeks anyhow, so you don't want to burden them with attachments they won't be allowed or even want to keep. Some have learned to look only forward because looking back hasn't been real productive for them. It's a fine line between nurturing and burdening. Like overwatering a houseplant. You don't want to do that or let it dry up, either."

I was looking blankly at this boy now, wondering what category he would fall into, the nurtured or burdened by our attention. Then Evie burst into the room, running with her short little wobbly steps on her ever-present high heels.

"Is that Primrose?" she squealed. "Oh, Primrose, look who arrived this afternoon!"

"Hi," I said finally, because this boy and I had been staring at each other as if we were on opposite sides of a window without benefit of sound.

"Hi," he said back.

"IT'S KED!" screamed Evie.

"Don't scream, Evie, you're going to frighten him," said Bert, shuffling in from the den.

"I'm just so excited," said Evie. "Primrose, this is Ked Schneider."

And Ked looked down and gave her the kindliest possible smile. It's amazing, I thought, how some people come through such things with their kindliness intact. He didn't look like you might expect, sullen or snappish or feral.

"Now let's go sit and have some iced tea," said Evie. "I've told Ked all about you."

"Mostly you're what she's talked about since I got here," said Ked shyly. "You were in foster care too."

"Yep," I said, but I was thinking, Well, I was in *Evie's and Bert's* care. It was almost impossible to think of them generically.

We all sat down but we couldn't think of anything to say next. Bert rescued the situation by hauling me to the bathroom and showing me how he'd started to recaulk the bathtub. I could see he was doing a very good job of it and keeping a straight line, which, he explained, is hard to do. There was a small bedroom that was Ked's now and I noticed that the door was closed and I was betting that Bert or Evie had closed it to give him the dignity of a private room that people didn't go barging into uninvited. They had done the same for me when I'd lived with them in Nanaimo.

After I'd complimented Bert on the caulking we went back to the living room with our iced tea. Everyone's glasses were sweating because Evie kept the heat up pretty high in the double-wide. The glasses were dripping a bit and I had to keep putting mine down on the napkin provided. I could tell that Ked was worrying about leaving rings on the coffee table because he kept picking his up and surreptitiously wiping where it had been with his napkin. It showed he had been with somebody who had taken the trouble to teach him not to leave wet rings on other people's furniture. Finally his napkin was all wet and he took the corner of his hoodie and wiped the table, making it look like he was just reaching his hand to his glass and the hoodie happened to follow. I wanted to put him out of his misery by letting him know the table wasn't real wood but I couldn't think how to say anything without calling attention to the whole thing and making it worse and Evie was in a state of high excitement and didn't notice and Bert had gone to the kitchen to get some pretzels.

When he got back we all reached for one and Ked and I bumped hands.

"Sorry," we said at the same time, and dropped our pretzels. We didn't even bother retrieving them for fear of another collision and no one went for the pretzels after that. The whole thing was getting painful.

Ked had bangs that fell over his eyes so even though

we were both shy he had a place to hide. I kept putting my iced tea glass up against my forehead and in front of my face as if my face needed cooling. I slipped surreptitious looks at him from behind it. When the silence began to stretch on a little too long Bert said, "Well, if we've all had all the pretzels we want, shall we go off to dinner?"

Everyone stood up so quickly it was like we had springs in our rear ends. We wasted a little time shuffling awkwardly to the door and such while Evie looked for her cardigan and then her purse and then her keys and then her raincoat because it had started to rain. Ked had a light Windbreaker, which was clearly going to be useless in Coal Harbor. We don't get a smattering of rain; it pours down like the deluge and penetrates all but the most professional-type rain gear. We looked awkwardly at his thin little jacket and then Bert decided we should drive over even though it was only a shortish walk and we never normally would have. But Evie and I cottoned to the plan right away and got in the car like it was the most natural thing to drive six blocks while I wondered what type of parents bought you a thin little Windbreaker to get through a West Coast winter. Or maybe he hadn't had parents in a long time, just a series of foster homes where no one wanted to spend money on his outerwear. Evie had told me they never quizzed the foster kids. If they wanted to volunteer information they would. Most of them came with so little they could call their own, starting with any say about where they got placed, the least you could do was allow them their privacy and dignity.

"'Cause none of them have very pretty stories to tell or they wouldn't be here and sometimes I think even to themselves they like to tell it different than it was. Or believe it will turn out different than it probably will," she'd explained to me.

When we got to The Girl on the Red Swing it was only four-thirty. Even Evie and Bert usually waited until five to eat. We all sat in a booth and stared mutely and intensely at the menu as if the secret of the universe were contained on those plasticized pages. Bert and Evie weren't usually shy but if you asked me it was the sheer size of Ked that was striking them dumb. I think they had looked forward to having a cockapoo in human form and patting him on the head like a lapdog, but they'd need a ladder to reach the top of Ked's head.

"So," said Miss Bowzer once we'd introduced her to Ked. "What will you have?"

"Whatever you have, it comes on a waffle," I explained to Ked, because nowhere on the menu does it announce this, and some things, while appealing on their own, gross people out when they come waffleated. Even though you can drag the waffle out and pretend it's not there. But Ked just said, "Cool."

While we waited for dinner we didn't talk much. Evie

and Bert sat as they always did, side by side in the booth so they could sample things off each other's plates without reaching. That meant Ked and I shared the other side, which felt vaguely too intimate for having just met. We had to work to keep our legs and arms from accidentally brushing.

By the time our dinners came, Evie had recovered her sangfroid and kept us entertained with her endlessly sprightly chatter, full of gossip about everyone in town. I finished my French fries (which I always regard as more of a first course) and dug into my Welsh rarebit, which, by the way, goes excellently on a waffle—all that cheese just oozes into those waffle pockets. Figuring out what works particularly well on a waffle is part of the art of ordering at The Girl on the Red Swing. It had taken me a year of staring at Welsh rarebit on the menu before I finally ordered it, because Miss Bowzer wrote it as *Welsh Rabbit*. I don't know if it was a misprint or if that's how she thought it was spelled. It wasn't until I started helping her in the kitchen that I saw it being made and realized there was no actual rabbit in it; it was basically melted cheese and beer and now it's a favorite. It always makes me feel vaguely rakish too, because of the beer, and even though I know the alcohol cooks out, still, you are ingesting it.

As I was glorying in its cheesy goodness and beery daring, the restaurant door opened and a big man with black slicked-back hair and a big black Fu Manchu mustache that hung down both sides of his face came bursting in. Everyone turned to look at him, partly because he was so big and partly because he wasn't from Coal Harbor. Occasionally we get people coming into town who don't live here. We even have a motel. But usually they come in the summer. And the ones who are dressed as well as this guy don't stay at the motel and eat at The Girl on the Red Swing, they stay at Miss Clarice's expensive B and B out on Jackson Road and we don't see them because they're there for some peace and quiet and expensive buffalo-mozzarella-saturated meals. So we all gaped except Ked, who didn't know the difference between townsfolk and strangers and just kept scarfing down his cheeseburger, unaware there was a floor show.

It might have been an uncomfortable moment for the stranger, coming in to get a bite and having everyone stop breathing at the sight of him, but he didn't seem to mind. He was broad-shouldered and red-faced from the icy rain that had started and he dripped all over the floor by the front cash as he looked for the hostess to come seat him. He stood like an actor who has come onstage, exuding some kind of natural charisma and stage presence, and I thought any second he would break into a thrilling soliloquy. It was certainly an attention-getting way to be. We had lots of time to study it because Miss Bowzer was in the kitchen. She cooked, waited tables and hostessed.

Actually the latter wasn't much of a job as most people came in and just sat where they always did. But this stranger didn't know that so he took the PLEASE WAIT TO BE SEATED sign seriously and just stood there. I suppose somebody should have told him he could sit down but he seemed so totally in command of the situation that I think we all felt it would be an impertinence.

Eventually Miss Bowzer came from the back with a tray full of people's orders, and didn't seem to notice him until he said, "Kate!"

Miss Bowzer looked up, saw him and dropped her tray. Salads and waffles flew everywhere.

I'm sure all of us wanted to break into applause, although naturally we didn't. We should have gone back to eating our dinners but we didn't do that, either. Miss Bowzer, paying no attention to the broken plates and salad dressing underfoot, but treading unheeding over it all, walked up to him, and did a very peculiar thing. She poked him with one finger. One quick poke as if to make sure he was real.

"You came back," she said finally.

"Yes, I did," he said. "Or so it seems."

And then, because I realized who he must be, with his villain's look and slicked-back hair, I let out a little gulping sound. Ked studied me for a second and then studied Miss Bowzer and the man, who were now walking to the kitchen like they'd been planning this rendezvous for years.

We didn't see either of them again. Ked gave me another look and I knew he knew I knew something. But though he looked interested and curious, he didn't say anything.

Then again, no one in the whole restaurant was saying anything. *Anything at all.* It was like a restaurant of mutes. The people whose salads had been ruined looked ruefully at them and a man finally broke the silence and said, "You don't think she expects us to pay for those, do you?"

It echoed through the restaurant. I felt for the woman whose husband it was. She was probably always shushing him at Christmas parties and stuff.

"Oh, Bernard," said his wife. "You're such a *man*."

"And at such a moment!" added another woman sitting with them.

"What moment?" asked Bernard, looking completely flummoxed.

But the woman just sighed and a lot of other women, as if holding it in until someone got it started, also expelled long breaths and Ked looked at me and we laughed. Then before the laugh could become too companionable, he cut it off and returned to his dinner as though someone were going to come and yell at him for laughing. He was attacking his cheeseburger with such voracity and guilty intensity that I wanted to say, For God's sake, all you did was laugh. But instead I went back to my dinner with equal companionable voracity. I hoped he realized that this was for his benefit and didn't think I chowed down like this all the time.

Everyone else went back to eating too, but there was a hushed quality now and if you asked me, people were keeping it down because they were straining to hear any snippets of conversation from the kitchen. When Miss Bowzer still didn't come back out, people started getting quietly up and leaving money for their bills on their tables. One woman needed change and asked her friends to make it, and when they couldn't, they went back to the kitchen and never came out either.

I knew there was a door from the kitchen onto the street but Ked didn't. "Bermuda Triangle," he muttered to no one in particular, and I laughed and he looked all wary again.

"My goodness, I guess they plan to stay back there forever," said Evie, who was still cutting and chewing but whose eyes had never left the kitchen door. "I wonder who he is."

"I think I know," I said.

So I told the story and she and Bert thought it was very romantic until they pulled themselves together and realized that this made Dan Sneild my uncle's rival and how I might feel about it. Then they frowned and *tsk-tsk*ed but I could see their hearts weren't in it. Everyone enjoys a good love story and this certainly stepped things up a notch in the saga of Miss Bowzer.

Ked just politely kept chewing. He had dragged his waffle out from under his cheeseburger when it arrived and now, done with the burger, he was pouring syrup all over his waffle and eating it as a second course, which showed he understood the concept perfectly.

"Well, it's too bad about Miss Bowzer and this, uh, visitor," said Evie, never taking her eyes off the kitchen door. "Because she makes great pies, don't she, Bert?"

"Nobody makes a pie like Miss Bowzer except perhaps Evie," agreed Bert.

"Aw, Bert. Anyhow, Ked, we wanted you to try some pie. We wanted you to order *three kinds of pie*!"

"At least!" said Bert.

"But it looks like everyone's packing it in. I guess we ought to go too so Miss Bowzer can have a nice visit with that young man who looks like an otter," said Evie, and then her eyes darted guiltily to me and she added, "Or not such a nice visit. Usually seeing someone after all those years all you have is an awkward old time, finding you never knew what you saw in the person so long ago. Don't you think, Bert?"

"I've never had such an experience, I guess, Evie," said Bert.

"But you can guess that, right?"

"That's what I'd guess," said Bert firmly, and then got up to pay the bill.

By now, Mr. Barrista was manning the cash register so

people could pay and get out without bothering Miss Bowzer.

Evie and Ked and I were heading for the door when this old guy everyone calls the seer grabbed Ked by the sleeve and pulled him over to his booth. Ked didn't know yet that you don't want to get corralled by the seer.

The seer is an old fisherman who sits in The Girl on the Red Swing all day and drinks coffee and mutters to himself. Once when I was helping out, Miss Bowzer wanted me to pour him more coffee, but I admitted that he scared me. He'd been sitting there as many years as I could remember, just getting older and shaggier and weirder. If he can, he engages you in conversation about his dreams. To hear him tell it, he dreams every night about everyone in town. He thinks the dreamtown is real and that it's important we all know what he sees us doing there. The first time he told me about this, I told Miss Bowzer I thought he was crazy and she said, "Oh, he's just a little addled after all those years alone at sea. The ones who go out alone for long days and nights, they get funny in the end."

"My dad fishes alone!" I said.

"He's got you and your mom, for heaven's sake. Harry's got no one at all. That's probably why he's invented this whole dreamtown. He doesn't see folks much in his real life. But in his dreams he's got a life full of everyone's comings and goings to keep track of. And it don't hurt no one to listen to what he sees. You know we none of us can stay entertained with just our own life. We gotta be kept up to date with a bunch of different lives and what's happening in them. That's why TV's so popular, I guess. But who's Harry got to keep track of? No one. So he keeps track of us all. Everyone feels better with a job and I guess he thinks that's his. And if people don't listen, he never bothers them twice."

That was more or less true but the part she left out was that when people politely but firmly stopped the seer's rambling dream narratives, his eyes followed them the rest of the time they were there, watching them eat, like he knew stuff they didn't and felt sorry for them, not being able to see what was coming. Well, if that didn't give you the willies I don't know what would. And who wants to know their oncoming sorrows? Even if they're only imagined, haven't you got enough to deal with in the here and now? But there he was telling Ked stuff, and Ked seemed riveted.

I went to wait with Evie and Bert, who were in the alcove next to the gumball machine.

"Gumball?" asked Bert as I approached. He handed me a nickel and one for Ked, too. But I hung on to Ked's nickel, since putting it in, turning the knob and waiting to see what color you got was the best part. The gum itself only had flavor for about three minutes.

"Look at that boy!" said Evie. "He's listening so politely to Harry rambling on."

"He's such a nice boy," said Bert. "You can tell that straight off."

"And not frightened like some by the hair."

The seer has a matted beard and mustache and long matted tangled hair. He looks a little like a dog that hasn't been groomed.

I could see the seer going on and on and Ked seemed frozen. It began to occur to me that Ked wasn't being polite so much as he simply wasn't capable of moving on. This, I thought, was an unexpected bonanza for the seer. Someone he could corral who didn't know how to disengage himself.

"Someone better rescue him," I said to Bert and Evie.

So Bert went over and told the seer we had to go.

I gave Ked the nickel for his gumball. He looked a little embarrassed and self-conscious but he got the gumball as it seemed to be expected of him and then we ran out to the car in the pouring rain. Dripping in the backseat and trying to keep our forming puddles separate, we stared ahead into the foggy downpour.

"Now, Ked," said Evie. "You don't have to have anything to do with that man in there. He's a nice harmless old guy but he's kind of wrong in the head, if you know what I mean. Next time just say good night and move on."

"I didn't know," said Ked.

"We're not blaming you, we just want you to know," said Evie.

"What did he tell you?" I asked, unable to restrain myself.

"He said to tell you he saw you sitting on a platform in his dream last night. And you were all alone. He said to tell you it was important."

"Me? Oh, that's so creepy," I said. "And he thinks *everything* he dreams is important."

"He don't know nothing, darling," said Evie. "Not more than the rest of us. He gets lonely. Most people just ignore him."

"I try to buy him a cup of coffee or lunch now and then," said Bert. "He don't have much and he's too proud to sit here all day without paying for something to eat."

"Even though Miss Bowzer would let him," said Evie. "Because she's got a good heart that way. He knew her dad, who was a fisherman too. But he won't take her charity. He tells people their futures or what he sees them doing in the dreamtown, in exchange for a meal. Some people listen to him just to make sure he gets fed."

"The last time I talked to him he said that people shimmer up over the town like light reflected off water. That's how he sees everyone so clearly. He watches the reflections," I said. Even though I don't want to hear the seer describe things that probably aren't true, I do like his idea of everything shimmering above, able to be seen by all of us if we look. He might have been a poet if he'd been a little more on planet Earth and a little less crazy. All that shimmering talk reminded me of a Mary Oliver essay where she watches a turtle die. It was my favorite of all the things Miss Connon had given us to read and I had memorized the last bit. "Not at this moment, but soon enough, we are lambs and we are leaves, and we are stars, and the shining, mysterious pond water itself." So maybe that is what he saw shimmering, our shining mysterious pond water selves. But I didn't share this because it's not the type of thing you spout off when you're in a car with someone you've only just met.

"Well, that's mostly nonsense talk, that shimmery stuff," said Bert.

"It don't mean nothing unless you *want* it to mean something. These things never do," said Evie. "Don't give it another thought."

"He says he sees it all in his dreams. That he sees what happens next. It'd be nice to know what was going to happen next," said Ked. Then he flushed again, as he seemed to whenever he thought he'd shared something terribly personal. I got the feeling he wasn't used to being included in normal speculation.

"Sees it all in his dreams? We all do, honey," said Evie. "We all see it all in our dreams. It don't mean it's true. Now let's go back to the trailer for some ice cream."

So we did, and over the ice cream I shook off the willies a bit. Of course because we were at Evie's house the ice cream had mini marshmallows in it. They didn't improve the ice cream but they didn't hurt it either and I thought that was what you could say about most things. Although I couldn't quite get to the kernel of that idea, the feeling of it made me happy because it meant in a way you didn't have to sweat and work so hard to improve things and fix things and you couldn't much ruin them either. You could change them but that was the most you could do. It kind of took the pressure off your time on earth. Mini marshmallow theory of life.

"What did the seer say about *you*?" I asked Ked, pretending to be busy with a marshmallow.

"Oh, he didn't really say anything," said Ked, but I could tell he was lying. "He told me to tell you about that platform, that's all."

"What does he mean a platform? Like a stage? Or a train platform?"

"I don't know," said Ked. "I didn't think to ask."

"I guess it doesn't matter because I don't believe in his dreams anyhow."

"I guess I don't either really," said Ked, but he looked off and ate his ice cream in such a way that I got the feeling he did. Or at least wanted to. And looking at him, I was curious. Some people you meet and it's like they're a door you go through. In and out and that's that. And sometimes you meet someone and they share everything about themselves, give it up so quickly and fully that you know there's nothing left to mine for there, it's all on the surface for you to see. But sometimes you meet someone and it's as if they're this whole biosphere and you want to go in and roam around and find out what all is in there—as if it's so rich and plush a space you'll never find all the animals living under the ferns. No matter how much you roam and look, there's always going to be more interesting stuff hidden in the depths, microbes and reptiles and plant life and mammals and things you couldn't even guess at.

I finished my ice cream and went home to tell my mom about Dan Sneild coming to town and see if she was worried about him stealing Miss Bowzer from Uncle Jack because let's face it, Uncle Jack hadn't put himself in a very solid position.

"Oh, old boyfriends," she said, shrugging. "She's probably more curious about him than anything."

But lying in bed that night, I worried.

Welsh Rabbit

In a saucepan over medium heat whisk two tablespoons of melted butter with two tablespoons of flour.
Add one teaspoon dry mustard and one teaspoon
Worcestershire sauce and some salt and pepper. Stir
in one half cup of dark beer. When this is smooth,
add three quarters of a cup of cream and then two
cups of shredded sharp Cheddar cheese. Serve over
toast or a waffle. It is especially good with waffles,
and if you call it Welsh rabbit you may get to eat the
whole thing yourself.

What Happened on Jackson Road

THE NEXT MORNING WHILE sitting in class, I wondered how Ked was doing on his first day in his new school. At lunch, Eleanor asked me if I wanted to go to her house later and I gave a vague answer because I wanted to sniff around The Girl on the Red Swing and try to find out why Dan Sneild was in town and how Miss Bowzer felt about it. But I wasn't sure if Miss Bowzer would be okay with this or consider it an invasion of privacy. I mulled this over during math. When the bell rang I had pretty much decided on Miss Bowzer, not Eleanor, when I saw Ked hanging from the monkey bars on the playground. He was so tall that he had to bend his legs from the knees and even then his knees almost hit the ground. The junior high got out an hour before us so he had obviously made his way over to our school. I wondered if it was to see me or if he was just wandering around checking different places out.

"Hi, Ked!" I called.

He let go of the bars and dropped onto his shins.

Eleanor came outside and raced up to me. "Who's that?" she asked in my ear. I wiped it. How did she manage to exude so much stickiness without even touching you?

"It's Ked," I said.

"How do *you* know him?" asked Eleanor as we walked over.

"I just met him. He's new in town," I said, deliberately not answering her question. I didn't want to say he was Bert and Evie's foster child. As soon as people find out someone is a foster child they treat them as if they are criminals or diseased. One thing I learned when my parents disappeared at sea was that it is human nature to secretly suspect that the things that happen to people are really their own fault in some way. That we bring our misfortunes upon ourselves. Even if the bad things that happen to us are clearly just a case of bad luck, there's a kind of underlying belief that there's a certain amount of bad luck in the world and it attaches to people who are less deserving. I wanted to protect Ked from this even though it was probably something he already knew.

"Hi," I said as we approached him.

"So, Primrose, are you coming over to my house or what?" asked Eleanor, completely ignoring Ked.

"No, I think I'll show Ked around."

"Why don't we take him to the hockey game? He'll meet guys his own age there, and then you and I can go back to my house," said Eleanor.

Ked and I both looked at her blankly for a moment. I realized we were talking about Ked as if he were an inanimate object or a dog. Something to pick up and put down where we chose. But there was something in his air that was a little like that. As if he weren't quite in the same hemisphere as the people he was with.

"I *could* take you to Uncle Jack's, I guess," I said.

Uncle Jack's house used to belong to the navy and had a gym attached to it. He leaves the house open so that the kids who want to play street hockey after school can get into the gym.

"If you want to play hockey, there's always a hockey game there," said Eleanor, without turning around.

"I don't have a stick," said Ked.

"Maybe one of the guys has an extra," said Eleanor. She probably wanted to find an excuse to peek in on Spinky, who played there every day.

"We could tell Evie and Bert you need a stick," I suggested.

"No," said Ked, and he looked so damply uncomfortable, for a minute I thought Eleanor's condition was contagious. "I don't want to start asking them for stuff."

"Well, you could buy one, then. They carry them at the hardware store," said Eleanor.

"I don't have any money," said Ked.

"Do you *play* hockey?" asked Eleanor, but she pronounced each word slowly and distinctly as if he spoke a foreign language.

"I like ice hockey," said Ked, and then looked embarrassed, the way he always did when he made normal conversation but seemed to think he'd just revealed something daringly personal.

"This is just street hockey," I said.

"What's the diff, come on," said Eleanor in her bossy way, and marched ahead toward Uncle Jack's.

Neither one of us seemed to have a response to this so we just trailed behind her.

"Eleanor," I said to her back. "Do you think your mom would give me her recipe for red Jell-O pistachio salad? I'm writing a youth cookbook."

"No," said Eleanor. "She would *like* to but that recipe has been in our family for six hundred years. We are sworn never to give it to anyone."

"Has Jell-O been around for six hundred years?" whispered Ked as we continued to plod along after Eleanor.

"Of course not," I said. "Oh well, even if she gave it to me, she'd probably insist on half the profits from the book or something. I want to write and publish a cookbook for real. We have a lady in town who makes money writing cat books."

"There's a lot of money in cats," said Ked.

"Oh, I know," I said. "Our bookstore/gift shop carries

cat pillowcases and pot holders and stuff. You know, if you wanted to edit the cookbook and help collect recipes, I'd share the money with you. I'd rather do it with someone than alone. But not Eleanor." I whispered this last.

"I don't know how to cook," said Ked.

"Well, I can teach you," I said. "Miss Bowzer taught me. I know how to chop like a real chef. I can show you if you want. Then we can try out recipes together." *Finally*, I thought, someone my age I can chop with.

"Hurry *up!*" barked Eleanor, who had reached Uncle Jack's and was heading inside.

We followed Eleanor. There was a game already in play and Ked didn't even go into the gym but hovered in the doorway with me. Eleanor, confronted with so much running testosterone, lost her bossiness and just sat on a side bench mooning over Spinky. As though drawn by her magnetic, if psychotic, gaze, Spinky, who was standing on the sidelines, came over and sat beside her.

"What's that foster kid doing here?" Spinky asked. Clearly the news had made the rounds of the boys.

"He's a foster kid?" asked Eleanor, giving Ked a surreptitious look.

Both Ked and I acted like we hadn't heard.

Then she said, "Gross."

"Let's go," I said, and walked out, pulling Ked with me. "Spinky's really an idiot."

Ked didn't say anything.

"Eleanor, too," I said when we had gone down the road a bit. "Mostly you'll find Coal Harbor full of nice people."

Ked still didn't say anything, but what *could* he say?

"But there's still, you know, your usual idiot percentage. Kids used to throw stones at me when my parents went missing. They don't do that anymore. If people throw stones at *you*, they'll have to deal with me."

Ked laughed. When I looked surprised he said quickly, "No offense, you just don't look like much of a threat."

It is true that I am of a small, delicate frame, but I am very wiry. "You'd be surprised," I said with dignity. I remembered how when the kids threw stones at me, Miss Bowzer suggested getting Uncle Jack to kick the crap out of them and although one believes violence solves nothing, it was nevertheless comforting to know that some grown-up was willing to step in and make such a politically incorrect suggestion. This was when I first knew I liked Miss Bowzer. I was a little alarmed to find myself making such rash offers of protection, but it is very hard not to pass on the things that people have done for you that have been helpful.

"I don't want to make waves. I can just avoid them," said Ked.

We walked a bit in silence. We were heading toward town but I didn't know where we were going. I wished I could take him someplace peaceful and then I thought of Jackson Road and the viscosity of its stillness. I know some people are unaffected by it but I didn't think Ked would be. I once biked there with Eleanor but I would not do that again. All she did was chatter relentlessly about Spinky. She managed to dilute the viscosity of Jackson Road with her incessant noise so that by the time we reached its end it was as thin and watery as everywhere else.

"Do you want to bike somewhere with me? My uncle has a bike you could borrow, I bet. We just have to go to town to ask him. But first let's go to my house and get my bike and test-run a recipe. Would you like the first recipe in our book to be freeziola or ersatz gravy?"

In the end, Ked didn't seem to have a strong preference so I picked ersatz gravy because it was fast. Ked learned quickly. In fact, so quickly that I began to suspect he had more than a passing acquaintance with the kitchen and wondered why he pretended otherwise.

After that, with the afternoon quickly disappearing, we charged over to Uncle Jack's restaurant. Ked wanted to stay outside on the sidewalk because he said it would be awkward if Uncle Jack didn't want to lend his bike. But I knew he would say yes, so I dragged Ked inside.

I found Uncle Jack covered in a thin film of plaster dust and looking irritated the way you are when you are breathing in things you shouldn't be.

"Primrose, it's not a good idea to come in here. Plaster and drywall keep falling from the ceiling." As if to illustrate, a big chunk dropped down a few feet behind us.

"What the heck!" Uncle Jack roared, turning his head. Now all our heads were turned toward the window and we saw something even more disturbing. Miss Bowzer was standing in the door of The Girl on the Red Swing saying goodbye to Dan Sneild with a *kiss*. It was only a peck on the cheek but I was still appalled. I had never seen Miss Bowzer kiss *anyone*. I, frankly, didn't know she had it in her.

Ked started coughing and I tried to introduce him to Uncle Jack but it sounded as if Ked were choking to death and he finally had to go outside to get out of the dust.

"That was Ked. That person over there being *kissed* is Dan Sneild," I said with the secret thrill you get from being the bearer of news, even, or perhaps especially, bad news. "He used to be Miss Bowzer's boyfriend and now he's back in town. I haven't found out why but when I do I will tell you."

"No need," said Uncle Jack. "I'm not keeping tabs on Miss Bowzer and neither should you. What she does is her own business. And this isn't someplace you should be without a hard hat."

So then I told him about Ked. "And can he borrow your bike when he needs one?"

Uncle Jack looked distracted as more plaster fell like snow. He headed for the stairs and called over his shoulder, "It's locked in the garage. Key in the change jar on the kitchen table."

I was turning to leave when I saw one of Miss Bowzer's restaurant bowls on a window ledge. You could see the remains of red sauce in it, covered in a thin film of plaster dust.

"What's this?" I called, holding up the bowl.

"Miss Bowzer brought over some salad dressing," he called out over the stair railing. "She gets stranger and stranger. She came racing in and practically threw it at me. All she said was, '*VINAIGRETTE*. In case you didn't know, it's *FRENCH*!' She's very mysterious, that woman, Primrose."

"Some people find mystery alluring," I called back. "I'm sure Dan Sneild does!"

I went out to rescue Ked, who was now being swarmed by a bunch of dread-headed Hacky Sack players who had appeared out of nowhere and taken over the sidewalk. One of them grabbed the corner of his jacket and said, "Save the Mendolay mountain, man."

"What?" said Ked.

"Dude, you don't know?" said another. "Come on back to our tents. We're set up outside town. We gotta tell you, like, what's going on."

They started to pull on Ked and he looked alarmed. I was pretty alarmed myself. You're not supposed to go off with strange guys who tell you to come to their tent.

"I got things to do," said Ked nervously.

"We have to go," I said to the Hacky Sack boys. I tried to make my voice firm, the way you do when you're talking to dogs. This was to ward off any of the attempts they might make to throw us into burlap bags and drown us in the river. I knew this was probably just a flight of my imagination but I think it is better to be prepared in such instances than not. Then I wondered why *burlap* bags? Whoever saw burlap bags nowadays? Was it because I had read about trolls taking people off in burlap bags in some old fairy tale written when people actually used burlap bags? Or was it because guys who looked like these were usually very environmentally conscious and wouldn't think of using plastic? So does one's mind meander even when in precarious on-the-verge-of-getting-kidnapped situations. It's surprising sometimes that our species has survived at all.

Fortunately the boys moved off down the street as I was pondering all this and they resumed their game without any further kidnapping attempts. I was slightly disappointed to have such peril fizzle out so quickly.

"Maybe we should stop at the sheriff's and tell him there are some strange guys in town trying to make people come to their tents," I said.

"I won't go to the sheriff's," said Ked.

This was the most definitive statement I had heard out of Ked. "Why?"

"I just don't like sheriffs," he said, and shrugged.

"All sheriffs?" I asked. "Because ours is very nice."

"Never mind the sheriff, what did your uncle say about the bike?" asked Ked.

"OH! He said you could borrow it, of course. Let's go get it and we'll bike out to Jackson Road and I'll show you Mendolay Mountain. Maybe we can figure out why they want to save it."

"They were probably just stoned," said Ked.

I turned back to look at the Hacky Sack players. I had never seen anyone stoned. I was a little shocked at this suggestion. Of course we had an antidrug program at school so I knew about such things but it was the type of thing I imagined happening in big places like Vancouver. Had drugs come to Coal Harbor?

"Do you really think they were stoned?"

Ked shrugged. "Didn't you notice their pupils? They were huge. I'm surprised they could hit the Hacky Sack."

This was a new one on me. Clearly they had more detail-filled drug programs where Ked came from. "Did you see stoned people in other towns where you lived?"

"Sometimes," said Ked. "Can we go to Bert and Evie's so I can drop off my books?"

I nodded.

"I'm going to run." And just like that he dashed down the street. I hoped this wasn't one of his quirks. I am not a fan of sudden rapid movement. I hopped on my bike and followed.

• • •

When Ked put down his books and told Bert and Evie where we were going, Evie tried to fill us up with fruit salad made with mini marshmallows. I didn't want any but Ked ate two big bowls of it.

"It's a good thing you like mini marshmallows," I whispered to him when she left the room.

"I don't," he whispered back. "But she thinks everyone does and she just wants to make you happy by putting them in everything. This morning she put them in my cereal."

And again I wondered how he had come through these years with such kindliness intact. We did Irish myths this year and learned that the Irish believe there are thin places, neither here nor the beyond but bordering between the two, and in these places dwell banshees, female ghosts that keen, which is a sort of high-pitched wail they make before someone dies. Ked wasn't a banshee because he wasn't a female and I didn't see him going around portending deaths. But, I thought, he's not really among us. That's how he's kept his kindliness. He exists in the thin places. He hovers there. He floats.

I knew these places from when my parents had disappeared and I felt I floated, not quite in touch with people who had lives in gear on planet Earth. It was like he was an outline of who he was but the substance was not available to anyone. I knew now that I could ask him questions about himself and his life but I wouldn't get answers. He was keeping himself safe and apart someplace where nothing and no one could quite touch him.

When I was in the thin places I was so hardly on Earth that I was accident-prone and consequently kept losing digits and little pieces of myself. I wanted to keep a hand on Ked and keep him safe. Especially because I wasn't sure that anyone else had ever really seen that he was in the thin places. I think you had to have been there to recognize it in someone else.

Ked, whose mind must have been elsewhere too, didn't even ask me why I was so suddenly silent but rinsed his bowl and put it in the dish drainer. And then we went to Uncle Jack's to get his bike.

In Uncle Jack's kitchen I had to dig around the endless toonies and loonies in the change jar on his table and finally tip it out to find the key. I bet Uncle Jack had thirty or forty bucks in change alone. He must be very partial to gumballs and parking meters, I thought. I found his bike helmet on a hook but Ked said he didn't want it.

"Wearing a helmet to ride a bike seems so arbitrary. You could hurt your head tripping on the sidewalk or as a passenger in a car. You know?"

"Oh, I completely agree! We have endless lectures about bike helmets during gym. It always strikes me as odd that the people who give you lectures about wearing helmets are all too happy to help you snap your neck by forcing you to do somersaults and backflips and balance one-footed high up on things you've no business crawling about on to begin with."

We hopped on the bikes and headed out to Jackson Road, where there is so little traffic, you can bike down the center without worrying. A horn tooted behind us suddenly and we had to veer to the side to avoid a fancy black car that whizzed by. It was Dan Sneild, who must have been going back to the B and B, where he was staying.

"I hope he got his fill of French food," I said bitterly, and Ked laughed and laughed although he couldn't possibly know what I was talking about. "What?" I said. "What's so funny?"

"I don't know. It's just the way you say things," he said, and laughed again. When he laughed he didn't look so distant and floating. For a second you got a glimpse of who he would be if he were with you totally.

This made me want to say something else hilarious because really, Eleanor had never even gotten my jokes, much less appreciated them, but of course then I couldn't think of a single amusing thing to say so I decided to impress him with my knowledge of local lore instead.

The scenery had been typical West Coast island, old-growth rain forest—covered mountains, dense and deep, full of moss and lichen and ferns, but now we approached the cleared rolling hills of the farm. We stopped our bikes to admire the emerald fields.

"They didn't even *have* bulldozers when this land was cleared," I said proudly, as if I'd done it myself tree by tree with my teeth. Miss Bowzer had told me the whole history of the B and B, so for once I had some useful information to impart that I actually remembered. I do not have the type of brain that stores information well. I can glean concepts and imagine stuff but when I have to store any facts they go in one ear and out the other and I cannot recall them in the kind of coherent detail necessary to make sense. So it often appears that I know nothing at all, which is both embarrassing and untrue. Therefore I was quite pleased that I might actually be able to come up with some useful information like normal people seem to be able to. "Miss Bowzer told me the whole history of the B and B. It started off in the eighteen hundreds as a farm. This couple, Jed and Margaret Mason, built a log cabin and owned eighty acres that they had to clear to make a dairy farm. Jed died but Margaret kept the farm going anyhow. Then, in middle age, she meets and marries this millionaire."

"Where do you meet and marry a millionaire alone out here?" asked Ked.

"I don't know." To be honest, this had never occurred to me and the fact that it immediately struck Ked made me realize how smart he was.

"Anyhow, so she meets this millionaire and he turns her humble farm into a big ritzy estate and buys all the surrounding acreage so now they've got fifteen hundred acres and they have big parties and he breeds horses and she's supposed to be this socialite but really, she just wants to be a farmer so during dinner parties she's always racing out to help deliver calves and stuff. That's my favorite part of the story—the image of her running from her chandeliered dinner table in a gown and long gloves to help birth some calf. She got the reputation of being some kind of madwoman because she was always coming back for the next course covered in blood and hay. But she didn't care. That's why I like her. She cared more for doing the things she loved than what people thought of her. She could wear the tiara and velvet because she loved her husband and wanted to accommodate his socialite ritzy needs and she could get her dress torn to shreds rescuing a laboring cow. She didn't find the two things incongruous at all."

"What are those black animals out there in the field?" Ked asked, pointing.

"Buffalo. Miss Clarice's raising water buffalo and making mozzarella but we're not at that part of the story yet. So Margaret keeps the farm going alone until her death in the 1940s. The people who inherited it tried to sell it for a thousand dollars but no one wanted it. Can you believe it? My mom said that Miss Clarice paid eight hundred thousand for it so someone would have made a lot of money if they'd bought it for a thousand. Anyhow, Miss Bowzer wants it desperately. It's always been her dream to own it someday. It's all that history. I think it should go to someone who grew up around here, you know? Someone who has the love of this land in their bones. My mom said that in her family they had this rule about the stuff in their house. She grew up in this beach house that everyone in her family loved. She said they all loved everything about it, the dishes, the tablecloths, the vases, the pictures. And when someone moved out, if they really wanted a piece, they got to take it if they were the one who loved it most of all. Loving it most of all was kind of a claim to ownership."

"So Miss Clarice owns all these mountains?"

"No, she just bought the original cleared homestead. The surrounding mountains were bought by Blondet and Blondet Logging."

"Uh-huh," said Ked, squinting his eyes and looking over the large orange sun sinking behind those protective mountains. "Well, better enjoy it now. That must be why those guys are camped outside town. I've seen it happen in other places I've lived. Mendolay Mountain is going to be logged."

Raspberry Vinaigrette

If you are going to learn how to cook, it is important to learn basics like salad dressing. Some people make their own mayonnaise, but this is taking things too far. This raspberry vinaigrette is as easy as it gets. Put a third of a cup of olive oil, two tablespoons of raspberry jam and two tablespoons of raspberry vinegar in a blender or a shaker of some kind. Blend or shake it vigorously. Voilà. Do not serve this to gentlemen. When they see fruity salad dressings wending their way toward them they get very, very nervous. I think they secretly believe it will lead to pecans.

Eleanor's Family's Ultrasecret Six-Hundred-Year-Old Recipe for Red Jell-O Salad with Pistachios

Well, I suppose we'll just all have to guess.

What Didn't Happen at Miss Lark's

W E RODE ON MORE or less silently after that. In town we split up. Ked took the bike back to Uncle Jack's and I went home. I was surprised to find my mom already there.

"You got home early," I said. "Ked and I were just on Jackson Road but we didn't see your car pass, just Dan Sneild's. Ked thinks Mendolay Mountain is going to get logged."

My mom was stirring something on the stove and looked distracted. Her face suddenly clouded. "Yes, I heard there may be a clear-cut in the works and some people have come to organize a protest. How could a decent human condemn our mountains this way? And I don't like that Dan Sneild. I think he's up to something. Where did this ersatz gravy come from?"

"Ked and I were here earlier. I'm teaching him how to cook."

My mother just nodded. She seemed really tense and annoyed.

"You don't mind, do you?" I asked.

"No, it's not that, Primrose," she said. She banged around in the cupboard, looking for something. She was banging a lot harder than strictly necessary. "I got a letter back from Miss Honeycut. She doesn't want to use the money to help the Fishermen's Aid."

"Why not?"

"I have no idea. It was a *form* letter."

"She rejected you by form letter?"

"Well, clearly she anticipated a lot of requests." My mom crashed a pan lid down on a pot.

Dinner was surrounded by the cranky darkness of my mother's bad day.

"Really, John, what could be a fitter thing to do with that money? If she doesn't want to help the fishermen's families, how does she think she *can* help Coal Harbor?"

"Who knows?" said my father. He was eating his soup.

"Well, even if she got a lot of suggestions for using those funds, none could possibly be as suitable as this if she really does want to do something for the town. After all, fishing *is* the town. I just don't understand."

My mother stayed in her dark mood the rest of the night, but I could not be drawn in. I had my own worries.

"Honestly," said my mother to herself as she and I washed the dishes. She banged the counter with her fist and a plate bounced off and crashed on the floor.

"Don't worry," I said, picking up the pieces for her. "I have a feeling everything will come out fine in the end." It had occurred to me that if the mountain was clear-cut the view from the B and B would be ruined and that wouldn't be good for business. Maybe Miss Clarice would even sell it. But would Miss Bowzer still want it without a view? Still, despite all the protesters gathering, I couldn't believe anyone would strip all the trees from these mountains. They felt as much a part of who we all were as the ocean. They were members of the town, silent, but just as full of life. They had been standing for hundreds of years. They would be here hundreds of years more, I was sure.

"Well, as much as I'd like to believe in your feelings, Primrose, what the fishermen's families need is cold hard cash. I should write Miss Honeycut again. Maybe my first letter wasn't strong enough. I should tell her about the Harrison family, with no money coming in this winter and five mouths to feed. Their oldest boy is talking of quitting high school and getting a job on one of the boats and I think Mary's entertaining letting him. They have to eat. And what does Miss Honeycut mean, 'Thank you for giving this matter your attention but I prefer to explore other options'?" asked my mother, rereading

Miss Honeycut's letter and waving it around. "What other options? Who else has written to her?"

She looked forlornly at the broken dish as I swept the china crumbs into the dustpan. "And as far as I'm concerned she owes us a plate!"

My mother stomped off to knit and I could see by her furrowed brow that she was tied up in knots over her impotence to save all the lost fishermen and their families and ease the tide of suffering in her corner of the world. "Money, money, money," she said. "A little bit of extra money can fix an awful lot in this town. It all seems to hinge on a little bit of money."

"My grandmother used to say it's not a real trouble if it can be fixed by throwing money at it," said my dad from behind his paper.

"It is if you can fix it with money but you don't *have* the money. Those unfortunate people just need a little cash to feed those children through the winter!"

"And they're darned lucky to have you looking for it," said my dad.

"Well, it won't do them much good if I don't find any," said my mother. Then she got up for pen and paper and sat down to write Miss Honeycut again.

• • •

My mother wasn't the only one writing Miss Honeycut. The protesters had gotten wind of the Honeycut fund and were hoping to secure it to launch a full-scale protest against the logging. And it wasn't just the Hacky Sack kids who came to town after that. There were some older professorial types and environmentalists and a whole lot of other people. The motel filled up quickly and some of the protesters were billeted about town. None of them seemed to be the type who could afford rooms at Miss Clarice's B and B and when she was asked to donate some housing she refused. This surprised nobody.

The protesters did presentations in the schools to gain student support. They wrote our member of Parliament to protest the clear-cut, and the Hacky Sack kids tried to get as many people in town as they could to sign the letter.

Miss Connon posted the letter on the bulletin board during recess and when I went to add my name, she put a hand on my shoulder and said, "The poor, poor trees," and there were tears in her eyes. I found this a little unsettling. Seeing your teacher cry is like seeing one of your parents cry. But she quickly wiped her eyes and said, "Don't mind me, Primrose."

In their school presentation the protesters showed us that even if the trees were replanted, the forest would never come back the same. When trees die naturally and are allowed to lie where they fall, they rot and the rotted wood seeps nutrients back into the soil so that the forest replenishes itself constantly. The protesters showed pictures of small trees growing out of the fallen large trees, something I'd seen many times but never really thought about. You cannot re-create an old-growth forest. Once it's gone, it's gone. But really, they didn't have to get so scientific. Just the thought of the surrounding mountains treeless was enough to galvanize all of us into action. So I volunteered to collect signatures.

After school Ked and I met at my house to continue working on recipes for the book.

"What do you think it should be called?" I asked him.

"*Coal Harbor Recipes*?"

"Maybe something snazzier. We should go ask Miss Lark for publishing advice."

We got our bikes and rode out but when we got to her house, Miss Lark opened the door and glared down at us. Ked quickly took two giant steps back. Miss Lark was wearing a large man's mackinaw over a nightgown. Her feet were bare. She had a stocking cap on even though she was inside.

"What?" she barked.

"Hi, Miss Lark," I said. "I'm Primrose Squarp. This is Ked. You came to our class. I thought you might remember me."

"I don't know what class you're talking about. I go to a lot of places," said Miss Lark.

I thought this very odd but I forged ahead anyway. Nothing ventured, nothing gained.

"Miss Lark, we're writing a book," I began. "And we need some advice."

"Don't!" she barked, and slammed the door.

"Do you think we should ring the bell again and ask if she wants to sign the petition?" I asked, because I had brought that, too.

"No," said Ked, turning around and walking back to the bikes. "I don't want to collect signatures. I'll ride around with you while you get them but I don't want anyone to *see* me doing it."

"Why not? There's nothing wrong with it."

"It makes me nervous, okay? In my last foster home I was helping to build a set for our school play and I accidentally bonked a teacher with a piece of wood I had over my shoulder, and he immediately thought I was 'becoming violent.' If you collect signatures, you're aiding the protest. If I collect them, I'm looking for trouble."

I don't think people in Coal Harbor are that narrow-minded but I guess he had a right to be nervous. I couldn't imagine getting picked up and plunked down, never knowing what was going to happen next. You can't make permanent friends, you can't make plans, you can't join teams. And why was his home available to him and then unavailable? What was the deal with his parents? He must have had some if he went home between foster homes. Was he from a family of *career criminals*? I was sure I had heard of such things. I knew I shouldn't pry into his life but I was so curious. I cast around for a question that wouldn't be too intrusive.

"Do you think you'll be in Coal Harbor long?"

"I don't know."

"I bet Evie and Bert would keep you permanently if they knew you wanted to stay."

"Well, I don't," he said tersely.

This floored me. "Don't you like it here?"

"Yeah, I like it, Primrose. I like it a lot, but I've got things to do elsewhere. You know, responsibilities, people counting on me."

"But you must hate just going from place to place."

"I don't mind so much." He shrugged. "I'd like to know how long I've got places, though. That would help."

"Can't you ask?"

"It depends on forces beyond my control. Listen, I don't really want to talk about this anymore, okay?"

It is very odd to find yourself in the position of trying to help someone who has other plans.

Since we were headed to town, I decided to get signatures at The Girl on the Red Swing first.

"Hello again," said Miss Bowzer to Ked as we came in the front door.

"Again?" I asked Ked. "Were you here earlier?"

"I can't sign it!" interrupted Miss Bowzer when she saw the sheet. "I've had six people in here already asking."

"You don't want to save Mendolay Mountain?" I

asked. "But you love that mountain! The Hacky Sack kids say that once the loggers start, they'll do the whole coast."

"Scare tactics," said Miss Bowzer. "Listen, the logging company is only planning on that one mountain. That's it. I know that for a fact. And that's jobs for loggers, too, you know. It's fine to say they should stop logging but that's practically the whole economy of B.C. Anyone think of that? Besides, Dan's staying at the B and B and he says he doesn't think the clear-cut will much affect the view."

"But the B and B *faces* Mendolay. Its porch looks onto the mountain."

"Yes, Primrose, but there are *other* mountains. Mendolay is only *one*. A little clear-cut will get lost in the vast range that the B and B faces. I doubt you'll even notice it. *Dan* doesn't think people will."

I looked at Miss Bowzer as if she were from the moon. I never expected her to be on the side of the loggers. Never in a million years. And what did *Dan* have to do with it? Maybe the torturous choice between Dan Sneild and Uncle Jack had fragmented her brains.

"Anyhow, I've got pierogies to make. It's pierogi night," she said.

"*PIEROGI* night?" I said.

"Dan's Ukrainian," she said, and shrugged.

She never changed her menu for anyone, except for the one dish she'd added for Uncle Jack. And pierogi night was a much more serious commitment than air-dried beef with lentils. She was devoting a whole *night* to it. Miss Bowzer must have fallen back in love with Dan Sneild! She'd probably want to become Ukrainian herself next! This was terrible! I tried to imagine Miss Bowzer in a long colorful dress and boots and a scarf, doing wild dances with a lot of other Ukrainians, as I had seen on TV once. Could Uncle Jack continue to love her through such a metamorphosis?

"I suppose now she's going to put sauerkraut in everything the way Evie does mini marshmallows," I said to Ked, who had pulled me nervously outside.

I had a vision of an all-Ukrainian menu and that reminded me that I hadn't passed on any fake French food comments from Uncle Jack in a while, and I told Ked to wait for me a second while I dashed back into the kitchen of The Girl on the Red Swing and said, "Miss Bowzer, by the way, Uncle Jack said that a real cook could make *coq au vin.*"

"*Coq au vin?*" Miss Bowzer put down the pork roast she was carrying from the freezer.

"Yeah," I said, and then dashed out. I decided it was best just to let this simmer.

Outside, Ked was standing where I'd left him but had been joined by Bert and Evie.

"PRIMROSE!" said Evie in her wildly enthusiastic way. Sometimes she reminds me of a puppy, the way she greets people. And then, as if to be sure he didn't feel left out, she added, "AND SHE'S HERE WITH OUR FAVORITE BOY, KED!"

She would adopt him in a heartbeat, I thought. What kinds of responsibilities could he possibly have that would keep him from living in Coal Harbor? That would send him back to the kind of life that kept jettisoning him into foster homes?

"What are you kids up to?" asked Bert. "We've been to the library." He hefted two big bags of books to illustrate.

"To use the Internet!" said Evie proudly.

"You went on the computer there?" I asked.

"We got some help from that nice librarian," said Bert.

"Ms. Andersen," said Evie.

"The one with the long hair."

"And the glasses."

"She showed us how. We were looking for cockapoo breeders."

"We found all kinds of sites."

"They're called sites. Like building sites, the places where you go."

"There's more breeders than you'd think."

"Are you getting a new dog?" I asked. This was surprising news because they were so broken up about Quincehead that I'd have thought it would take much longer until they were ready.

As if reading my mind, Evie said, "We know there will never be another dog like Quincehead."

"Evie thought if Quincehead ever died it would be years, maybe never, until she could get a new dog."

"That's what's so amazing," said Evie.

"Because we realized the big hole Quincehead left in our lives."

"And Evie said to me, Let's get a dog."

"But that's when we decided to do lots of research first."

"Because Quincehead was a fluke."

"We didn't research or nothing to find Quincehead. He just fell into our lap and he was the perfect dog."

"We'll never see his like again."

"Not in this lifetime."

"So it's only fair to try and find a nearly perfect dog."

"Because it wouldn't be fair to the *dog* if we didn't."

"He's got so much to live up to as it is."

"So we'd even drive to Alberta to get a perfect one."

"How can you tell if it's the perfect dog before you know him?" asked Ked.

"Ked's so smart," said Evie to me.

"He hit the nail on the head. He's got us there, Evie," said Bert. "You can't."

"You can't tell at all," said Evie. "Not really."

"But you can guess," said Bert. "We'd be guessing, really."

"We just feel, you know, compelled to do our best," said Evie. "To find perfect candidates and then visit them. I think I could tell if I picked one up."

"You could tell with Quincehead, Evie."

"Because he snuggled into me. First time I picked him up."

"He snuggled."

"Not that the perfect one might snuggle next time."

"Not that there will ever *be* a perfect dog again. But we owe it to the new dog to get one nearly perfect."

"Because of Quincehead."

"And his perfection. Now, what are you kids doing in town?"

"We were going to get my uncle's signature on this petition to save Mendolay Mountain," I said.

"We're going to the council meeting after supper. That's on the agenda. We'll see you then. Are you going inside with Primrose?" Bert asked Ked.

"Because I thought we'd have an early supper," said Evie. "So we have time to digest before the meeting. I'm making Tater Tot casserole."

"I'll go back with you," said Ked, and he took both book bags from Bert, who looked frankly relieved. Bert was pretty short and I imagine it took more muscle than it would a taller person to keep the bags from dragging on the ground.

"Does Tater Tot casserole have mini marshmallows in it?" Ked asked, rather nervously, I thought.

"It does if you want it to!" said Evie.

"Wait a second," I said to Evie. "Can you just stay here one second so I can get your recipe for Tater Tot casserole?

I've got my notebook. I'm collecting recipes for the cook-book Ked and I are writing."

So Evie stayed behind and I took down the recipe and Ked and Bert trotted home with the books.

After I had finished writing, I said, "Would you adopt Ked permanently if he wanted it?"

"Of course, Primrose. But you know, honey, that that isn't going to happen. He has a home. This is just tempo-rary."

"But don't you think he would be happier if he could just be in one place?"

Evie thought a second. "I'm trying to remember what the social worker said. She said he was actually anxious to get back to his own home."

"But what kind of home can it be if he's hardly ever there?" I asked.

Evie put her hand on my wrist. "Well, you know we've talked about these things before. Some of these kids are ashamed of their families. The social worker said Ked didn't want anyone to know about his family but she'd tell me anyhow if it would be a help to us and I said to her, 'Dearie, I don't need to know nothing he doesn't want me to know.' And maybe the way I think of it would help you, too, Primrose. I think of it as having this moment in time with him and doing anything I can. Maybe we're just like a vacation spot in the schedule of his life—like a little spa trip. Someplace he can be warm and dry and fed. And maybe part of that for him is being someplace where everyone doesn't know where he came from. Like we're a little vacation from shame. Anyhow, honey, I gotta go make dinner. I'm glad you're getting on so well with Ked. He needs a friend, that's for sure."

But that didn't even begin to cover my feelings about it. I wanted to keep him *safe*.

She moved on and I crossed the street and went into Uncle Jack's restaurant.

There were plastic sheets hanging all over the place and plaster falling everywhere and things didn't look any further along than they had the last time I'd been there. Uncle Jack was in the back, covered in white plaster dust and looking distracted and furious. I held the signature sheet out to him.

"Save Mendolay Mountain?" he said, signing it. "Sure, sure. You know that's on the agenda for the council meeting."

"Are you going tonight? Ked and I are."

"If I can get away from business. Right now, between the restaurant and a bunch of irons in the fire down island, I'm working sixteen-hour days," he said. "Hey, you and Ked haven't borrowed any change out of the change jar the last couple of weeks, have you?"

"No, I would have told you," I said.

"I know, I know," said Uncle Jack. He sounded tired and discouraged. "Maybe I'm mistaken but I could swear about a third of it is missing."

"Wow. Who would take all your change?" I asked.

"I don't know. I don't want to think one of the hockey players is stealing. It's not the change. It's feeling taken advantage of after I trusted them with the open door. I'd hate to tell them they can't use the gym anymore unless I'm around to open and close. I guess I'll have to talk to them. I don't want to make any accusations when I don't know anything for sure."

"What if no one comes forward?"

"I don't know," said Uncle Jack, and there were huge bangs from the back room. "Hey, watch it back there!"

"Miss Bowzer wouldn't sign the petition. She *wants* them to log the mountain!" I said. It was as well he knew what a pretty pass things had come to since he had neglected his courtship of her.

"Of course she'll sign the petition," said Uncle Jack, who was busy writing something on a clipboard.

"No, she won't. I just talked to her."

"She'll sign. She'll find somewhere to sign where it won't get back to us she signed."

"That doesn't make any sense. Why would she do that?" I argued.

"There's more here than meets the eye, Primrose," said Uncle Jack, and he winked at me. "But don't worry. I've got plans and I'm sticking to them."

I didn't know what to say to that. By plans, did he mean his restaurant? Did he mean he was going to keep building it even if it drove Miss Bowzer into the arms of

Dan Sneild? Didn't he see that she was worth more than a business enterprise?

I decided to try another tack. "Have you noticed that Dan Sneild is always eating at The Girl on the Red Swing?"

"People have to eat somewhere. I imagine he gets tired of the haute cuisine up at Miss Clarice's."

"She likes him."

"Miss Clarice?"

"NO, *MISS BOWZER!*"

"So I hear."

"They knew each other in high school."

"I knew a lot of people in high school, Primrose, what's your point?"

"Yes, but this is romantic."

"Is *it* romantic, or are *you?*"

"Well, somebody better be," I said meaningly. "Did you know tonight was *pierogi night*? Miss Bowzer never had pierogi night before."

"So?" said Uncle Jack, tapping on timbers and writing on his clipboard. It was getting on my nerves.

"Dan Sneild is *UKRAINIAN.*"

"It's a free country," said Uncle Jack, laughing.

"You'll be laughing out of the other side of your mouth when Miss Bowzer starts dressing in dirndls and making great vats of sauerkraut."

"I think you're confusing the Ukraine with Bavaria," said Uncle Jack, still scribbling away.

"Miss Bowzer thinks Dan Sneild might be here to buy the B and B. When they were younger it was their dream to own it."

Now he stopped writing.

"Miss Clarice's B and B?"

"Well, of course it wasn't Miss Clarice's then. Miss Bowzer has always wanted it. It's her dream."

"I thought The Girl on the Red Swing was Miss Bowzer's dream. She certainly gets prickly if she thinks it's been insulted."

"She's *proud of* The Girl on the Red Swing, she *created* The Girl on the Red Swing, but her heart's desire is the B and B! All her life she has wanted to live there. She spends all her free time decorating it in her head."

Uncle Jack put down his clipboard and looked at me straight on for the first time since I'd come in. "Well, well. Now, this does make things interesting. I've always thought a B and B was a two-person business." He looked thoughtful for a minute. I was hoping he would say something heroic like, Then there's no other choice—I will have to run Dan Sneild through with my saber, but when he finally spoke it was crushingly disappointing. "Let's hope she gets it, then. Everyone should have their heart's desire. You, me, even Miss Bowzer."

"*EVEN?*" I protested.

"Now," he said, shuttling me toward the door, "as much as I love these little tête-à-têtes, let's shoot you back outside while you still have a *tête*." As if to illustrate, a plank fell from the ceiling, and Uncle Jack bellowed, "WATCH IT UP THERE!"

Then he clapped me on the shoulder and pushed me gently through the door, saying, "Thanks for looking out for me, Primrose, but let's just say I'm not worried about that particular problem."

He had disappeared back inside before I could reply, but I was sorely tempted to say, Well, if you're going to get worried I'd advise doing so before the first of their twelve children is born.

Tater Tot Casserole

Brown a pound of hamburger with a chopped onion or two in an ovenproof skillet. You can add some chopped green pepper or red pepper or corn or other things if you like but my advice is not to make it too terribly vegetably or it loses its *je ne sais quoi*. Drain the excess fat off unless you *like* excess fat. Spread the hamburger mixture evenly over the bottom of the pan. Put half of a pound bag of Tater Tots on top. Thin a can of cream of mushroom soup with half a cup of milk and pour that on top. Then put one and a half cups of grated Cheddar cheese over all and bake the whole thing in a 350-degree oven for forty-five minutes. On a cold rainy night when people are not participating in the better plan you have for them, this can be a comfort.

What Happened at the Meeting

WHEN WE ENTERED THE town hall, I was still sulking. It is
very annoying to be putting everyone's life to rights
without any help from them or those around them.

There were long backless benches set out, which could
get very uncomfortable if the meeting dragged on too
long. My dad said once that he suspected that was why
they were used. My mom and dad and Evie and Bert were
down at one end of a bench with Ked and me at the
other. Miss Connon was sitting in the row in front of
me and waved to me cheerily as I came in. Miss Bowzer
didn't come at all, which was surprising. She usually closed
the restaurant early if there was a town meeting. But
maybe she had to keep it open all the time because, as she
had said, it wasn't doing so well. Or maybe she was embarrassed to come to a meeting where so many people

had signed a petition she refused to. You could count on most everyone showing up for these things. Aside from the movie theater, which only changed its movie every six weeks, it was, entertainmentwise, the only game in town. There was a loud buzz of excited conversation as people came in and greeted, like long-lost relatives, acquaintances they'd seen not two hours before. There was a kind of festivity to these gatherings that really called for cake. I looked around hopefully but apparently this was to be a pastryless event.

Dan Sneild was across the way, sitting with Miss Clarice.

"What's *he* doing here?" I whispered to Ked, who just shrugged.

Uncle Jack came in at the last second and squeezed in next to me.

"I thought you weren't coming," I whispered to him.

"I had to. I got a letter asking me to do something. It's not going to make your mom happy."

And then the mayor tapped the table with his gavel and we had to be quiet. At first it was very boring, with requests for dull things like stop signs and the removal of stop signs. It seemed to be a big concern where drivers should and should not stop. There was a contingent who wanted a series of stop signs put on the road that runs parallel to the beach because a lot of children and dogs like to run in that area and people use it as a speed course.

"Someday some child is going to get hit," said a woman indignantly.

"Or even worse, a *dog*!" said another woman passionately.

This occasioned a moment's silence while people tried to figure out if they'd heard right.

Then there was the usual uprising from the cat people, who didn't think cat safety got enough consideration, and there was even a budgie lover who spoke up, but nobody took her seriously. Finally, things appeared to be back on track. I always found these discussions like new fires. They fizz up and look really scary, like they might flame right out of control, but eventually they settle down to a quiet crackling hiss and then burn themselves down to embers.

This fire had appeared to die down and we were listening to the mayor raise the issue of parking meters when someone stood up and yelled, "ANIMAL HATERS!" and the mayor, who is a nice man, broke into a visible sweat.

It was for just such moments that we all came to the meetings. The topics under discussion often seemed largely beside the point. The point was to have an opinion and make sure everyone heard it. It seemed to me particularly necessary for people who lived alone and didn't have the benefit of someone always available on whom to force their views. They were always the most vocal. I pointed this out to Ked and he thought a minute and said, "Do they need to shout most because they have no one at home to shout at or do they have no one at home because they like to shout so much?"

I would like to point out that this was a fine point

Eleanor would *never* have come up with and it required some thinking through. By the time I had finished, the mayor had moved things from parking and pets to the "Honeycut Project," as he called it.

"It's been suggested to me that instead of overwhelming Miss Honeycut with a raft of letters, we unite to write her with *one* plan for the use of the money. That way the project will be chosen not so much by her but by a majority of *us*. Does that make sense?" asked the mayor.

There was a quiet buzz that seemed mostly favorable to this idea. It made sense to me. Who knows what strange notion Miss Honeycut would support if left to her own devices? She might choose the budgie lady's idea of starting a budgie sanctuary. We didn't want her blowing half a million pounds on *birds*.

The mayor got out a sheet of paper and began to read all the various ideas people had had since Miss Honeycut's letter had been published in the newspaper. Then people stood up to plead their cases. My mother made a stirring speech about Fishermen's Aid. A less stirring speech was made by the Hacky Sack kids.

Eleanor's mom stood up and said, "What do you people think you're doing, coming into town with your Rastafarian hair and wanting the money for some big global project that has nothing to do with Coal Harbor and just stirs up trouble?"

"Now, I don't want you folks to stand up and start

arguing and, uh, shouting and such," said the mayor, ing his forehead again when the usual twittering on the old-lady bench and a restless stirring in general had begun. "We have plenty of time to choose a cause, as this selection process has just begun."

That's when Uncle Jack stood up.

"Well, I'm afraid I have news that is going to eliminate the need for such a process, Eric." (That's the mayor's name.) "I'm sorry I didn't have time to get this on the agenda but I only got the letter today. As some of you know, Miss Honeycut and I were friends."

There was some sniggering in the audience. A lot of people were aware that Miss Honeycut had set her cap at Uncle Jack in a kind of sad and desperate way. He ignored the sniggering, although he turned slightly redder, but it was hard to detect unless you knew him well because Uncle Jack was always pretty red. He was so full of life that he glowed from within.

"Anyhow, I guess that's why she appointed this task to me. She has made me her agent over here. And it seems"— he cleared his throat—"that's she's *already* decided on a project."

"Well, THAT didn't take long!" my mother cried. "She couldn't have even gotten my second letter yet."

"We want a boardwalk!" screamed the little old ladies, banging their canes until someone in front of them said, "SHHH!"

on't you shush me, Young Man Having a Very
d Hair Day!" cried one of the old ladies, hitting the
shusher's chair with her cane.

The Hacky Sacks looked on in amazement. I don't
think they were used to old ladies outshouting them.

Miss Connon stood up and whispered, "That's so
mean, making fun of someone's *hair*," and walked out. I
saw her face and I could swear she was starting to cry
again. Lately she seemed to cry at the drop of a hat.

One of the Hacky Sacks, who was sitting right in
front of me, turned to a boardwalk granny and said, "I
know you don't like my hair but I think your hair is very
nice."

"I do it myself," the granny whispered to him.

"Really? I'd never guess. I was a hairdresser. I got fired
a few months ago. I was giving a woman a perm and I
sort of forgot about the time and her hair fell out."

"Oh my," said the granny, looking concerned. "That
would be worrying. But we all make mistakes, don't we?"

"That's not what the owner said."

"Now, don't fret, dear," said the granny. "You'll find
work again."

"Oh, I know," he whispered back. "I'm not doing this
just because I couldn't find a job, you know. I really believe in saving the rain forest."

"Of course you do!" she said, patting him on the knee.
There was a pause. "I could hire you to do *my* hair."

"I wouldn't if I were you. I think you're doing a lovely

job yourself. And to be honest, I'm kind of scared I'm going to burn off someone's hair again."

"We'll buy you an egg timer!"

"It's okay, really," he said, turning red.

They continued to whisper but I couldn't hear the rest of their conversation because the level of noise and chaos was escalating.

"Listen, folks!" shouted Uncle Jack over the roar, trying to get matters back on track. "It doesn't make any difference what you all want because Miss Honeycut has chosen a project that is dear to her heart."

At this there was an outbreak of groans.

"This money to allocate is Miss Honeycut's," Uncle Jack reminded everyone. "And it seems that what she's decided to do with it is build a park and erect a statue of her father in it."

At this there was dead silence.

It was broken by one of the fishermen shouting, "We don't want no stinking park with some statue of some guy we never even met."

"Yah!" piped up someone else. "What does her father have to do with Coal Harbor?"

"BOARDWALK! BOARDWALK!" yelled a particularly sprightly old lady in a lime-green pantsuit, trying to rally the troops, but they all looked exhausted. One of them looked like she was working on a stroke.

"It's true her father had nothing to do with Coal Harbor. Except leave us this money—which it would behoove us to use as Miss Honeycut sees fit. We'll still get a park. And a, uh, statue. We can, of course, refuse the money." Uncle Jack paused meaningly.

The room went quiet again.

"But I'm afraid it will do no good to try to persuade her otherwise. I took the liberty of phoning her as soon as I got the letter, explaining that feelings might be not completely unanimously in her corner on this one. But she made it quite plain that this is her intention and she won't be dissuaded."

"*Half a million dollars* for a park and a statue?" someone cried. "That's crazy! We don't have a piece of land *worth* that much!"

The room erupted into a blend of disappointed voices, bemoaning Miss Honeycut's lack of sense. Just like the rich, came up again and again. Just like *her*, came up even more often. I felt bad for my mom. She had come to the meeting, certain that she'd convince everyone of the need to give the money to Fishermen's Aid.

In the midst of this Dan Sneild stood up. "Excuse me. Excuse me, please, folks." He had to say it quite a few times before the room quieted down and he got everyone's attention.

"I know a lot of you planned to stop the clear-cut and create some kind of international appeal with Miss Honeycut's money but I have to tell you, it would do no good. We've got no plans to do some big wholesale clear-cut. We don't do that any longer. You folks are behind the times. We do a small area. In this case one small mountain, which we will replant afterward because our goal is always sustainable forestry. Now, you all need to help us find a balance between jobs for loggers and the needs of the community. This province was built on logging just the same as fishing. How'd you feel if some environmentalists came into town and closed down the fishing business? I suggest you all bow to the inevitable and remember those loggers are supporting families same as you folks are."

Well, I think he was doing okay until he told us to bow to the inevitable. About half the room erupted in angry cries and the other half, myself included, were stunned silent to find out that Dan Sneild worked for the logging company. A lot of us hadn't thought he was in town for any reason other than to win Miss Bowzer and talk Miss Clarice into selling the B and B. Now I understood why Miss Bowzer wasn't at the meeting. She could hardly protest the clear-cut being arranged by her *fiancé-to-be*.

"Oh, this is terrible," I said to Ked. But he didn't understand what I was talking about.

"No, it's demolition derby!" he said, his eyes sparkling as he looked from one hysterical contingent to the next. I could see his point. One dread-head had just beaned Eleanor's mom with his Hacky Sack. It had made a little dent in her tightly curled perm but otherwise didn't seem to have injured her. I thought he had crossed a line and felt bad for her until she got up and poured some cold tea on him. "Are these meetings always like this?"

"Well, people in Coal Harbor have strong feelings," I said proudly. "But I thought you didn't like altercations."

"I don't mind them as long as they're not about me. This is weirdly balletic, like a good hockey game," said Ked.

It *was* kind of lovely in its anarchy. It was a kind of ballet of desires. People wanted different things and there was something *nice* about wanting them and the noise and movement all swirling around those things.

"Miss Bowzer knows what Dan Sneild does for a living," I said to Uncle Jack. "She must! *That's* why she won't sign the petition."

"She'll sign," he said, and his eyes twinkled as he sat there implacably, as unruffled and unrufflable as always. He even looked passively on as Dan Sneild made a long speech about how the company was ecosensitive, using a lot of technical terms that I could tell no one understood. I figured that was probably Dan Sneild's intention. What he was probably saying in technospeak was, And then we plan to uproot and get rid of every last living thing on planet Earth.

Now would be a fine time for Uncle Jack to get up and punch Dan Sneild right in the nose. He could do it under the pretense of being ecosensitive himself. Everyone would approve. If Eleanor's mother could go around throwing tea on people, I'm sure no one would fault Uncle Jack for a jealous punch or two. But no, he just sat there calmly as Dan Sneild went on to say that even Miss

Clarice, whose property *faced* the mountain, wasn't going to protest it. "But perhaps it would have more weight coming from her," he said. Then Miss Clarice stood up and talked about how she had such faith that Blondet and Blondet was going to replant and make a new forest and log sensitively and responsibly, at which point one of the grannies dropped her knitting, stood up and shouted, "THIS IS CRAP!"

Mrs. Henderson, whom I knew to be quiet and well-mannered, started repeating "crap" like a chant. She was either finding a new freedom of speech in her old age or she had developed Tourette's.

Eleanor's mom put her hands over Eleanor's ears, which must have been very embarrassing for Eleanor and also useless, as the damage was done.

"Why didn't you tell the mayor first thing about Miss Honeycut's letter?" I asked Uncle Jack.

"I wanted to hear how people wanted to spend the money," said Uncle Jack, winking. "As a developer, you never know what kind of knowledge will be useful."

The mayor started banging his gavel. You could see huge wet rings under his arms. Some of the kids started balling up pieces of paper and throwing them, just for the fun of it. Some of the protesters burst into a chorus of "We Shall Overcome" and some others linked their arms and started swaying and singing, and in general people enjoyed themselves in whatever fashion took their fancy.

Finally the mayor seemed to give up, declared the meeting over and walked out. Which meant that effectively there was no meeting left, just a lot of people screaming at each other. So those of us not inclined to hand-to-hand combat or ululation put on our coats and left.

Evie, Bert, Ked and Uncle Jack all came to our house for the postmortem.

I took Ked into the kitchen and showed him how to make cinnamon toast. "The trick is to put lots of melted butter on the toast and then to make sure the cinnamon sugar melts into the butter." I demonstrated. "We could put this in our cookbook. Or do you think it's too easy?"

"Not if we call it *Recipes for the Simple-Minded*," said Ked.

Evie came in and proudly eyed Ked buttering toast. "Teenage boys have got such wondrous appetites," she said. "You want me to put some mini marshmallows on that, honey?" She pulled out the Baggie of them she kept in her purse for emergencies.

But Ked said it was perfect just as it was. It was, too. Cinnamon toast is so good I'm surprised we bother eating anything else. When Evie went back to the living room, Ked told me that because of Evie's belief in the appetites of teenage boys, he was eating way more than he wanted so as not to shake the foundations of her beliefs.

We brought a plate of toast into the living room as my mother was saying, "Honestly, Jack, why didn't you just tell Miss Honeycut to . . . stick it?"

"Look, Jane, we're going to get the money for the park

or no money at all. Who cares if she wants to erect a statue?"

"Oh, I'd just like to throw it up in her face and say forget it, keep your money. If she really loved the town, she'd know where that money would do some good. To her this isn't about the town, it's about coming back as some big shot who has a statue of her father in the square. Who needs it?" said my mother.

"I doubt you'll ever see her face in Coal Harbor again, but point taken. Well, I've been able to hive off a little anyway, which can go to the Fishermen's Aid or wherever the town decides it wants to use it. She's giving me seven percent, my usual realtor's fee for finding the property and purchasing it for her, so I'm going to give that back to the town. I would have said that at the meeting if that Sneild fellow hadn't interrupted."

"Thank heavens Fishermen's Aid will get *something*."

"Not necessarily. *I* can't decide where the money goes. I have to let the town make that decision. Even though technically it's my money, it's money that will come to me through Miss Honeycut, and you can see feelings are running high about the allocation of those funds as it is."

"I don't know why we have to let the town decide. I don't know why you can't just quietly give it to Fishermen's Aid."

"Because someone will find out and I have to live in this town."

"We still got some time to get people swayed to

Fishermen's Aid," said Evie. "Primrose and Ked can help. Can't you?"

"Sure," I said.

Ked looked up and said something nervously indistinct, his mouth full of toast.

"There, you see," said Bert.

Then everyone seemed to tire out from all the passion and excitement and my mom and Evie made more hot chocolate and Bert and my dad talked about fishing.

"Ked here wants to be a fisherman," said Bert proudly.

"Well!" said my dad. "Well!"

We were all silent, looking at each other and digesting this information or maybe just not knowing what to say next. Ked looked like he would like to crawl under his chair but he was frozen into a posture of politeness. Then you could see a lightbulb go on over my dad's head and he said, "Hey! Why not come out on the boat with me one Saturday?"

I thought this would be too much for Ked, who didn't like the spotlight—and when you're just two in a boat at sea, it's kind of hard to hide. But I was wrong because his eyes lit up like a pinball machine.

"That would be great," he said calmly, and I could see he was straining to appear cool and controlled to match my dad's demeanor.

"That would be great!" echoed Bert as if he were Ked's personal voice-amplifying machine.

"Well, okay then!" said my dad, and he looked happy

but surprised too, the way he always did when he'd some-how managed to do something useful for someone.

We continued to sit there staring in a happy, vacant manner. To be honest I was a little miffed that Bert knew something as important as what Ked wanted to be and I didn't. I thought if Ked was going to confide anything to anyone it would be to me, the person who really under-stood him and was watching out for him.

And then I had another sudden thought and turned to Uncle Jack. "I don't understand why Miss Clarice doesn't seem to care about the clear-cut. She's really the one most affected. Her business depends on the view."

"I'm going to make a prediction," Uncle Jack said. "And we'll see if it comes to pass. I'm going to predict that before long Miss Clarice puts that property of hers on the market."

My mother, who was coming in with a pot of hot chocolate, said, "Nonsense. She'll never do it. When she hired me she said she planned to live there until she died."

"Plans change," said Uncle Jack enigmatically, and re-fused to talk any more about it.

Did Uncle Jack already know that Miss Clarice was going to sell the B and B because he had put an offer on it? Was he buying it for Miss Bowzer after all? Or had Dan Sneild bought it and that was what he was hinting at? Who was going to get the B and B? Because it seemed to me that the person getting the B and B got Miss Bowzer thrown in for free.

"Why won't you tell?" I blurted out, interrupting Uncle Jack, who was talking to Bert now. "Why are you being so mysterious?"

They both stopped and looked at me politely.

"Because I don't know anything for *sure*, Primrose," said Uncle Jack. "And I don't want to start unfounded rumors. That's just a prediction. As reliable as looking in a crystal ball. The only reason I told you was because lately you've had this worried look every time I see you and I thought I'd give you something new and interesting to chew on."

I wanted to say, But you're one of the things I'm worried about. Dan Sneild is going to scoop up Miss Bowzer and that will be that. You will lose her forever.

Then, before I could decide whether to say this flat out, the party broke up and everyone started moving toward the door.

"Come on, honey. Let's go home and I'll make you a casserole," said Evie to Ked.

"But we already had supper," said Ked in alarm. "And cinnamon toast."

Evie looked crushed.

"But I could really use some fruit salad with mini marshmallows," he added quickly.

"Coming right up," said Evie happily.

Cinnamon Toast

Make toast. Butter it well. Make sure it's melty. Add a judicious amount of previously mixed-up cinnamon and sugar. Serve.

Gussied-Up Cinnamon Toast

Follow steps one and two. Add brown sugar and cinnamon. Run briefly under the broiler.

What Happened
at Uncle Jack's Office

A LOT HAPPENED IN the weeks that followed but the logging didn't happen as immediately as any of us had
feared. Dan Sneild stayed on at the B and B. The Hacky
Sack kids and the older environmentalists became a fixture and were busy trying to recruit people for the big day
when the logging began. They had to work really hard
because it's difficult to keep people whipped to a white-hot
protesting fury when nothing much is going on.

One day, seemingly out of the blue, Uncle Jack called
it quits with his restaurant and a big FOR SALE sign went
into its window, surprising everyone. His only explanation was that he was tired of renovating a building where
the darn ceiling wouldn't stay up. He had his eye now on
something else. But he wouldn't say what.

I tried to hint to Miss Bowzer that he had sold it

because he didn't want to displease her but she just gave me a skeptical look. You'd think someone in love with two men at once would be waltzing around with stars in her eyes but all she seemed was secretive and irritated. I told her that Uncle Jack said that she couldn't make *crème brûlée* and she said, "I'm not cooking any more French food, Primrose." And that was that.

Ked and I were making great strides with our cookbook. Every day after school we went to my house to experiment with recipes.

"We'd better publish this, Primrose," he said one day. "Because the cost of the ingredients must be beginning to add up. We should pay your parents back."

"Well, it's all just stuff we have around the house anyhow," I said, up to my elbows in biscuit dough. We were making buttermilk biscuits. "We're actually doing them a favor because this buttermilk is two days expired and would just get thrown out anyway."

We cut the biscuits out companionably. Ked was much more meticulous than I was and his biscuits looked perfect, while mine looked like they'd been nibbled round the edges by cats.

"I don't know whether to get arrested or not," I said for the hundredth time. One of the nice things about Ked was that he never minded how many times you repeated yourself while working through a problem.

Everyone in school was talking about the protest. The big exciting question for all the kids in Coal Harbor was whether or not we were going to let ourselves get hauled off to jail. It had been explained to us that if you blocked the road as planned, and were warned by the sheriff you were breaking the law by doing so and still wouldn't move, you'd be arrested. Even if you were twelve. Some parents wouldn't let their kids be arrested but many would, feeling that it was a moral decision that affected their future even more than the grown-ups'. My mom and dad said I had to make such a decision for myself. This disappointed me because I didn't want to go to jail any more than I wanted the clear-cut and was hoping they'd tell me I couldn't get myself arrested, so that any moral laxity would be on their part.

"They're going to clear-cut no matter what," said Ked.

"Maybe, but I think I should take a stand anyway, because it seems to me that when you look back on the Holocaust and stuff, everyone says, Why didn't they see it coming? Why didn't more people do something? It's so easy to notice and not do anything."

"Or to do things and they make no difference," said Ked.

"Or not to be able to think of anything to do," I said. Lately I lay in bed at night thumbing through what I could do for Miss Bowzer and Uncle Jack, what I could do for Ked, what I could do for the trees. Mostly what I could think of was nothing.

We pulled the biscuits out of the oven and tried a couple.

"These biscuits are boring," I said. "If we're going to include this recipe, we'd better play with it a little first. Add more butter? It is my experience that if you add more butter to anything, it improves it immeasurably. It is nice to have one simple solution that always works."

"*Simple Solutions for the Simple-Minded,* you could call the book that," said Ked. "I know what Evie would say."

"Add mini marshmallows," I said.

"Never fails," said Ked. "You could also call the book *Add Mini Marshmallows.*"

"We'd better leave that title for when Evie writes her own cookbook," I said. "How about *Just Throw Some Melted Butter on It and Call It a Day?*"

"Great title," said Ked.

"I was kidding," I said.

"I know, but it's a great title *because* it's such a bad title, you know?"

So that's what we called it.

• • •

Through all of the various happenings and troubles, the last person I expected to cause more trouble was Eleanor Milkmouse. I knew I had kind of left her in the lurch when Ked and I became friends. She didn't know that I'd come to some sort of turning point with her during the scissors incident, which had happened before I even met Ked. She thought I defected because of him, and whenever she could say something snide about him she did. One day during lunch she said to me, "Did I tell you that I'm going to your uncle Jack's office after school?"

Now that Uncle Jack wasn't working on his restaurant, he could be found a lot of the time in his real estate office.

"Why?"

"To tell him I know who has been stealing his change."

"How would you know?" I asked. "How do you even know someone *was*?"

"Because I talked to Spinky when I was helping him with the film projector and he said your uncle closed the gym for two days because his change was disappearing and then opened it again without any explanation. And I know who was stealing your uncle's money and I'm going to tell him and then I'm going to tell everyone."

"How do you know who took it?"

"I saw him."

"You saw him where?"

"At your uncle's, where else?"

"What were you doing there?" I asked.

"Spying on Spinky," she said. "If you hide under the kitchen table you can peek out through a hole in the tablecloth without anyone seeing you. I've lined the hole up with the door to the gym."

That she would hide under my uncle's kitchen table was one of the few things I'd ever found endearing about her.

"How long have you been spying on Spinky from under the kitchen table?" I asked. I tried to make my tone respectful because I could see it was something anyone in a lovelorn state might do.

"Long enough. Long enough to see Ked take the money. I knew he would steal. My mother said you're just asking for trouble, hanging out with a foster child."

Then the bell rang and she ran inside. I spent the rest of the afternoon madly passing notes to her, trying to convince her not to do this rash thing. Ked wouldn't have stolen the money. She had probably just heard him getting the key for the bike lock. I knew Uncle Jack wasn't stupid enough to just take Eleanor's word for it. But other people might not be so levelheaded. This was just the kind of incident Ked dreaded.

After school Ked was waiting for me as usual but all I had time to do was call out that I had to catch up with Eleanor and I'd talk to him later. Then I took off after Eleanor, who was speeding toward town on her surprisingly fast dumpy little legs.

Eleanor must have sensed that I might turn desperate enough to leap on her and stop her from going to Uncle Jack's, because she kept glancing back and speeding up whenever I got too close.

By the time Eleanor ran up the steps to his office and barged in without even knocking, I was two steps behind. My uncle looked up from his desk at our flushed faces in surprise. Then, as if sizing up the situation, he put his pen down and assumed a grave expression.

"Ked stole your money!" Eleanor blurted out. "I came over one day to, to, to . . ."

It was clear she hadn't thought ahead how to explain this.

"You came over to?" prompted Uncle Jack.

"And I was peeking through the window and I saw him steal it. Everything that was in the jar on the table. He dumped it out and put it in his pockets."

"He didn't!" I cried. "He wouldn't. You're lying."

"I'm not!" she said.

"You're jealous and you're lying!"

"I'm not. I wouldn't want to be with either of you. He's a delinquent and you're, you're CRAZY, like your whole family. My mother says only a crazy woman would go out in a boat in a storm and leave her child."

Oh, not this again, I thought, rolling my eyes. I'd had so much of this the year my parents disappeared that I was inured to it.

"Whoa, whoa, whoa!" said Uncle Jack, putting up his hands.

Eleanor and I pulled ourselves up short and stood panting for a second.

"Let's say," he said slowly, "that he did take this money."

"He DID!" shouted Eleanor.

"Okay," said Uncle Jack. "Even if I knew for sure he did, you know what I would do about it?"

"What?" breathed Eleanor eagerly, as if *now* we were getting somewhere.

"Nothing."

Her face fell.

"He didn't anyway!" I said.

"He DID!"

"Just a second, Primrose," said Uncle Jack, signaling me with his hands to be quiet. "You're both missing the point. The point is that it is information that would be mine to do with as I liked and what I'd like to do with it is nothing. So case closed. Nowhere to go with this. Thanks very much, let's all go back to what we were doing before this came up." And he picked up his pen hopefully.

"Well, if you don't do anything, I'm going to tell. I'm going to tell everyone and those boys will beat him up."

"Why would the boys beat him up?" asked Uncle Jack, putting his pen back down.

"Because he let you think one of them had taken it."

"In the first place, I don't know where you got your information but I let them know last week they weren't under suspicion and the matter was closed. So all of this is old news. To everyone."

"You *KNEW*?" asked Eleanor.

"Yes," said Uncle Jack.

"He never would. I don't believe it," I said. "If someone said he did, they lied. How could you tell the boys that Ked took it?"

"I didn't," said Uncle Jack. "No one knows anything, and that's the way it is going to stay. As far as I'm concerned, I misplaced that change myself."

"But you didn't, because I *saw* him," said Eleanor, and I could see she was simply insane by now, because never in her right mind would she argue this way with a grown-up. She was so out of character that any second I expected her to grab a pair of sharp scissors and wantonly cut up some paper. "Anyhow, you can't keep me from telling everyone the truth."

"Let me help you think of this differently, then," said Uncle Jack, again signaling with his hands for me to stay quiet, because I had opened my mouth, although even I didn't know what I was going to say this time. I was feeling almost as insane as Eleanor looked. "Think about all the children born into poverty and starving. I know you go to the Anglican church, Eleanor. Haven't they been collecting money to help children in Africa with AIDS?"

"Yes."

"Well, some of them still die, don't they? Really, lots of them. Because they're not as lucky as you."

"Yes," said Eleanor, but she still had on her insanely angry voice. I was kind of respecting how long she could keep herself stirred up. I didn't think she had it in her.

"And think of all the terrible things that happen to people. And to trees too. Is it the trees' fault they are to be clear-cut? People and animals and trees and everything alive are born into circumstances they have no control over. Bad and unfair things, undeserved things happen to them every day. And knowing this and how lucky we are, we feel so helpless and maybe a little guilty because by chance we were born into better circumstances. And we can't change that. We can't level the playing field. We can't make those circumstances not exist. But although we can't keep undeserved bad things from happening, we do have control in making undeserved *good* things happen. We can say, Maybe this person technically doesn't deserve that I give him a break, or look the other way, or let him get away with it. But I can. I have *that* power even if I haven't the other. You see what I mean?"

"No," said Eleanor.

"Is it fair that Ked has to stay in foster homes? That this is the childhood he is having?"

"Yes," said Eleanor.

"No, it isn't. Even you can see that!" I said.

"Really, Eleanor, do you think so? A good Christian like you?" asked Uncle Jack, and I could see by his slightly sarcastic tone that she was really beginning to annoy him, because Uncle Jack was never sarcastic. "Why is it fair? What did he do to deserve it?"

"Well, his parents—" started Eleanor, but Uncle Jack interrupted her.

"We're not talking about what his parents did or didn't do. We're talking about Ked and what he's got to contend with that none of us can change. Now, if he stole the money, does he deserve for me to let him off the hook? Is that *justice*?"

"NO!" said Eleanor, obviously feeling on much more secure ground now.

"That's right, if he stole the money, justice would say that he shouldn't be let off the hook. But I don't believe in justice."

"Huh!" snorted Eleanor, in a tone that implied that nothing he believed surprised *her*.

"Because if there was justice, he wouldn't have had the childhood he's had. Maybe we don't live in a just universe. Maybe we live in a universe where all you have control over is your own kindness. And as far as I'm concerned, the kind thing to do is to leave that poor kid alone. And think about it, that's quite an interesting little power to have. Get it?"

"No," said Eleanor.

I looked at Uncle Jack but he didn't look back at me. It was really quite an interesting idea and I wondered if he had come up with it on the spot. He was looking intensely at Eleanor, trying to bend her to his will. I could have told him he was whistling in the wind. Eleanor is one of those people who are normally incredibly wimpy, so it's really annoying to find just how stubborn they can be when their wimpiness should be working in your favor.

Her brow was furrowed and she looked Uncle Jack right in the eye. "I don't care. I'm going to tell everyone."

"Then you'll have to explain what you were doing at my house when you saw him. What *were* you doing?" asked Uncle Jack, looking innocently curious.

"I was . . ." She stopped.

"Were you there to see anyone in particular?" asked Uncle Jack. I didn't think he knew about Spinky. I was pretty sure I was the only one who knew about Eleanor's abiding love for him, but Uncle Jack was so much smarter than the average bear that sometimes even *knowing* how clever he was, he surprised me.

"I was looking for Primrose," said Eleanor stoutly.

"No, she wasn't," I said. "I know who she was there to see, and if we're going to be going around telling everyone things—"

"Never mind," said Eleanor hastily. "You're all crazy. You and your mom and your dad and your uncle. You're all cracked. I don't want to have anything to do with any of you." Then, before she slammed the door, she said to me, "You'd better keep your mouth shut."

"You'd better keep *your* mouth shut!" I called after her.

Then I sat down in the chair across from Uncle Jack and he got a box of bourbon biscuits out of his middle drawer and we silently ate about a dozen.

"You know Ked didn't take the money, don't you?" I said.

Uncle Jack looked at me for a long moment and then he said, "Of course, Primrose."

When I got up to leave he heaved a sigh and said, "I'm going to be gone for a few weeks."

"Where are you going?"

"Down island. I have a lot of business there. I've been

commissioned to hunt for some farmland around Duncan and I'm selling some holdings."

"This is the worst time to go," I protested. "Any second Dan Sneild could pop the question."

"I'm sure he will," said Uncle Jack, passing me the biscuits again. But now he had a twinkle in his eye. Did he *want* Miss Bowzer to marry Dan Sneild?

"Harumph," I said.

"I think he is certainly going to pop the question and I think the answer is going to be yes and it's part of the reason I'm going down island," said Uncle Jack.

"To escape?" I asked. "Because it will break your heart? Can't you fight for her?"

"Don't worry, I have no desire to compete for the same heart that Dan Sneild is trying to claim."

So that was final. Uncle Jack didn't love Miss Bowzer after all. I had been wrong all along and so had my mother. All that French food for nothing. My stomach felt like stone. Miss Bowzer would marry an otter and Uncle Jack would be lonely forever. I took another bourbon biscuit and crunched on it with sharp, cranky teeth.

Uncle Jack did the same and finally said, "That friend of yours, Eleanor, is kind of a pill, isn't she?"

I nodded and grabbed another bourbon biscuit. "I imagine she made up that lie because I kind of ditched her."

"Jealousy," said Uncle Jack, chewing ruminatively. "It's amazing how often people try to stir up jealousy. You're always lucky if it doesn't backfire. Read *Othello*, Primrose, it's a very interesting play. Shakespeare knew everything."

"I wasn't *trying* to—" I began.

"I didn't mean you. I was thinking of someone else. We're out of bourbon biscuits," he said, shaking the empty box. "Want a fruit crème?"

I was about to settle into emptying another cookie box with Uncle Jack when I saw Ked going down the street.

"I gotta go," I said.

Uncle Jack looked up but kept trying to open the fruit crèmes and nodded. He was very intent on getting to those cookies and when I left he had two jammed in his mouth. He was not going to want his second TV dinner tonight.

I ran outside and joined Ked.

"I passed Eleanor," he said. "She looked crazy and you wouldn't believe the look she gave me. What happened?"

"Oh, girl stuff," I said. "And I was just visiting my uncle. You know, popping in."

I am the world's worst liar, I thought. I didn't sound remotely like myself.

Ked glanced at me and I could tell he thought I sounded phony too but he just said, "Let's get the bikes."

We rode and rode without talking and the woods and hills passed by and I couldn't see how Ked could ever stand to leave this place. Why didn't he fight to stay here?

We rode so long that by suppertime my legs were shaky

with fatigue but it was as if he and I and the hills were all part of one thing, separate from other things on Earth. Just as my mother and father and I were part of one thing, separate from all else. And these small subsets within the universe, I decided, are maybe what people love best. Whether it is you and the ocean or you and your sisters or you and your B and B, your husband and children.

I was thinking about this after dinner while I did homework and my parents watched TV but it wasn't until I was in bed that night that I thought about Eleanor again, insane with jealousy because she'd been excluded from Ked's and my subset. Then I wondered who Uncle Jack *did* mean, if it wasn't me, when he was spouting off about trying to stir up jealousy.

• • •

In the weeks that followed, Ked and I rode out to Jackson Road every day to visit the trees while we could.

There were usually a few Hacky Sack kids on Jackson Road keeping an eye on the mountain. We also ran into them at The Girl on the Red Swing, where Miss Bowzer had taken to feeding them in exchange for help in the kitchen. The first night they came in, trying to pool their money to split a dinner, she said they could have the leftover chicken for free—she had cooked too much. They said it was nice of her but they were all vegetarians.

"I can't just let them starve, Primrose," she said to me. "They've got such big eyes under all that unruly hair.

They remind me of a miniature poodle I used to have. He was always covered in tangles with his eyes just peeking out. Of course, he was a meat-eater." She sighed.

So after that she devised a vegetarian chili that they loved. She always kept a big pot on the stove and we got used to seeing them walking in at any time and helping themselves. Because of their ragged clothes and dreads she said they all looked like war orphans. She started calling them the vegetarian war orphans and it stuck and a lot of us called them that too.

"Why are you helping them if you're on the side of the loggers?" I asked.

"People gotta eat," she said.

"I know it's none of my business but how can Dan Sneild clear-cut a forest that will ruin the view of the B and B that you both love?" I asked, trying to avoid the vegetarian war orphans, who were swirling around performing tasks that I used to. It was wonderful to have Ked as my best friend (even though I only referred to him this way to myself) but as a result I had lost my routine with Miss Bowzer, and these interlopers had filled the vacancy.

Ked elbowed me in the ribs. He hated it when I just came out and asked people things like this. He was the opposite of the vegetarian war orphans, who were like a strange nomadic tribe whose credo was "Stir up trouble." They seemed to be having so much fun with the protest,

I sometimes suspected they forgot what they were protesting and it wasn't the trees they loved as much as it was the life they had created for themselves, drifting from town to town, eating vegetarian, doing good things and enjoying the camaraderie of righteousness.

"There's lots of stuff you don't understand, Primrose," Miss Bowzer said, bustling around, directing her patchouli-scented army.

"You got that right," I said, and Ked elbowed me again. He dragged me outside and we walked down Main Street.

Then I remembered to tell him that my dad said the forecast was good for Saturday and he could come out on the boat. The last few Saturdays had been too stormy to take a beginner.

Ked suddenly looked so excited that I thought he might be sick so I took away the Baggie of penuche Evie had sent with him and which we had started munching.

"You could apprentice on my dad's boat and then be a fisherman yourself someday," I speculated, chewing Evie's penuche with effort. The stickiness between your teeth was good for contemplating such things. Like cows chewing their cuds. I always think cows must have many deep thoughts.

"Nah," said Ked. "I could never afford a boat."

"Sure you could. You save up."

"Yeah, right, do you know how much those things cost?" muttered Ked, looking at the ground. "If I ever get a boat, it will be a miracle."

I decided to see if Miss Connon could help me find a Mary Oliver essay that Ked would like. Maybe she could find something that would make him feel more hopeful. But when I got to school the next day there at Miss Connon's desk sat *MISS LARK!*

"Where is Miss Connon?" I asked.

"Be quiet and sit down. Be quiet and sit down, all of you!" said Miss Lark, and the second bell hadn't even rung yet.

When everyone was seated Miss Lark stood up in her large tan-colored tie shoes and ill-fitting plaid skirt. She wasn't wearing a mackinaw but that was the only concession she had made toward normal fashion. She was wearing gray stockings topped by *ankle socks!*

"Miss Connon will not be returning for the rest of this semester. I will be substituting," she began, when a boy in the back yelled, "You're that author! You can't teach!"

"Put your hand up if you have something to say, young man," said Miss Lark. "I was a substitute teacher for many years and out of the goodness of my heart answered the call to duty because otherwise, you might have had to wait for a teacher to be found down island, which would mean missing school days that would have to be made up *in the summer.*"

You could tell Miss Lark relished this prospect.

"However," she went on regretfully, "I have responded to the call of need and will take over until Miss Connon is herself again. If she ever is."

Well, you can imagine the furor this created. Everyone liked Miss Connon except for some of the parents who thought the books with big words she favored were inappropriate. It was a well-known fact that Miss Connon was always getting in trouble with various parents who thought she should make at least a passing try at keeping us stupid. But Miss Connon always said she had no patience with people who kept a white-knuckled grip on ignorance when any fool could see that if you didn't know a word all you had to do was LOOK IT UP. I noticed that Miss Lark was of the ignorance-is-a-terminal-condition school because she had taken all the Mary Oliver and Walt Whitman books from the free-time reading shelves and replaced them with Nancy Drew and Hardy Boys.

I told Ked all about this immediately after school.

"What can be the matter with Miss Connon?" I asked. "Missing a whole semester?"

"Maybe she has cancer," said Ked.

Then we spent the rest of the afternoon riding around and debating which illnesses you could get that would make you miss so much school. But it turned out to be one we hadn't even thought of.

• • •

"It's not cancer," said my mother at dinner. She'd been on the phone trying to suss out information. "She's gone down island for a little rest cure."

"She was just *tired*?" I said in disbelief.

"Yes. Teachers work very, very hard. She was tired and she needed some psychological help."

"She's *mentally ill*?" I asked in further disbelief.

"Oh, Primrose, don't be so melodramatic. Everyone needs help from time to time. Why don't you make her a card and I'll mail it tomorrow."

And then my mother changed the subject.

That night after my mother thought I was asleep she gave my father the lowdown.

"Complete nervous breakdown. That's what Ruth, whose sister Joan teaches with her, says. Joan says people kept finding her crying in the teachers' lounge and doing odd things like forgetting to bring her lunch and spending the whole lunch hour staring into space. Well, no wonder, John. She had the care of both elderly parents, her disabled sister and all that teaching. You know, teaching is always hard. Giving, giving, giving. So much going out."

"It ranks second below air traffic controllers for burnout rate," said my dad.

My mother rattled on as if she hadn't heard him—the way she does when she's all excited to relate something. "And she didn't have enough coming in. I think that's what did her in. You have to have a balance, John. It can't all be outgoing. I wish there was something we could do for her. Primrose liked her so much."

"Who is taking care of the parents and sister?"

"A cousin came up to lend a hand."

"Well, then it sounds like her bases are covered."

"For now, but I wish something wonderful would come into her life. That's what she needs. She needs incoming. To restore some balance. She needs something good to happen to her. Out of the blue! Do we know any nice single men, maybe?"

My father laughed and then their voices faded as I drifted to sleep, thinking of all the books Miss Connon had found for me.

• • •

I set my alarm clock for four a.m. Saturday and ran to Bert and Evie's. My dad had gone down to the docks and I had told Ked I would meet him at his trailer and walk with him there. But when I got to the trailer, I found out Bert and Evie were planning to come too. This was such a big day for Ked. Evie had her Polaroid camera and kept snapping pictures of him: Ked leaving the double-wide on his first day of fishing, Ked leaving the trailer park on his first day of fishing, Ked between Bert and me on his first day of fishing, Ked taking a bite of a muffin with mini marshmallows as we walked down to the beach on his first day of fishing. She kept ripping off the Polaroids and showing them to me as they developed.

"It's so nice to have these mementos of the occasion," she said conspiratorially to me. "Men don't think about commemorating the occasion—not the way women do—but they're glad afterward. I'm going to make a scrapbook for Ked. And I'm going to macramé a nice cover for it and attach some seashells."

And I thought again how perfect Evie and Bert would be as Ked's adopted parents. How Evie would always be macraméing things for him and how Bert would keep him company at guy things. How he could join a sports team finally because he would know he'd be around the whole season and Evie would bring snacks with mini marshmallows to the game and no one in the whole world would be prouder of a son than they would be whenever he did anything noteworthy like take his next breath. My dad would teach him to fish. And maybe he would tell me I was his best friend and I would say, Isn't that funny, you're my best friend too, and afterward everyone would know. And maybe we'd be friends for life and many years from now be the two old-timers who sat in The Girl on the Red Swing and dawdled over our coffee and young people would come to us for stories about the way things used to be in Coal Harbor.

Evie had dressed for the occasion in her highest red heels so it took us a long time to make our way down the graveled forest road that went from the trailer park to the dock. Halfway down the road we heard barking from within the trees and a second later a fierce snarling dog leapt out at us.

"Oh my goodness!" shrieked Evie, immediately

lunging for Ked and trying to throw her little body in front of his huge one.

Ked looked down at Evie in his sleepy way and smiled.

"Whose dog could that be, Primrose?" asked Bert.

"I've never seen it before," I said.

"It looks hungry," said Ked, gently moving back in front of Evie.

"It looks like it hasn't been fed in a while," said Evie, pushing her way back in front of Ked.

"It's got burrs all over it," said Ked. "Maybe it's feral."

He moved back in front of Evie, which put him just a couple of feet from the dog.

"You stay away from it, Ked," said Evie. "You never know about stray dogs. It could have rabies."

But the ferocious dog just started whining in a sad, plaintive way and before Ked thought or any of us could stop him, he had knelt down to give it a piece of mini marshmallow muffin and the ferocious dog made a sad little cry and put its head on Ked's knee. Despite the fact that the dog was mud and burr covered, Ked picked it up like a baby and held it and fed it the rest of the muffin.

"We can't just leave him here, can we?" said Ked when it was determined the dog was a him. "He's so thin. You can see his ribs."

"I guess we can't leave it, can we, Bert?" said Evie.

"It don't look too terribly feral."

"Well, it looks *a little* feral," said Evie.

"But it don't act feral."

"It isn't feral at heart."

"Only in appearance."

"But good gracious, we got to get to the docks. You can't keep Primrose's dad waiting. Bring it along, Ked. Bert and I will take care of it while you fish."

Ked carried the dog because he had no collar or leash, and we hurried down to the docks. When we got there, Ked handed him to Bert. The dog looked a little frantic to see Ked going off toward my dad's boat and for a second Ked looked at him with worried eyes but Bert said, "Come on, Evie, let's go get it something to eat."

"And drink."

"And a leash and collar."

"We should go to the SPCA with it."

"Just in case someone is missing it."

"He appears to like mini marshmallows."

"Well, who doesn't?"

I ran up to see if I could engineer some conversation between my dad and Ked, sort of get the ball rolling because they are both so shy, but I needn't have worried. There was clearly a kind of kinship in their love of boats and the ocean. My dad had gotten started teaching Ked how to lift anchor and they both looked at me like I was a mosquito, so I dashed back to shore.

I wasn't used to getting up at four a.m. so I went back home to sleep for another three hours and by the time I returned to Bert and Evie's, Evie had gotten most of the burrs out of the dog's hair and had brushed it. She told me she had been feeding him little bits of hamburger all morning.

"It don't seem right just calling him Dog the way we been doing, though," said Evie.

"He might already have a name," said Bert.

"So we don't want to confuse him with a new name."

"But Dog don't seem friendly."

"How about Pooch?" asked Bert.

"That's not much friendlier. That's not so far from Dog," said Evie.

"But a little bit."

"Well, a *little* bit, Bert."

We took the dog over to the SPCA, where he barked and snarled at everyone. And the woman behind the desk didn't seem too eager to take him from us so Bert said, Well, if no one was looking for him, he guessed he'd just take him home until the owner showed up.

"Thank you," said the woman behind the desk, looking at Pooch with distaste, which made me want to bring Pooch home and make a nest for him away from these people who only liked beautiful well-behaved dogs. "As you can see, we're full up right now. We'll call you if we hear anything."

Evie tacked up a Polaroid of Pooch on the SPCA bulletin board and we headed to town to buy him the essentials.

"He's not the world's friendliest dog," said Evie as he snapped and snarled at everyone we met.

"He's no looker," said Bert.

"Even with the burrs out."

"Ked likes him."

"You can tell."

"Why don't you adopt him?" I asked suddenly.

"We're going to," said Bert.

"If no one claims him, of course," said Evie.

"No, I meant Ked," I said.

"Primrose, honey, you keep asking but we don't get that choice. He's not ours to do with what we like. Now, we don't know particulars, but we do know that others have got prior claim."

"Can't you even *ask?*" I said. "Don't you *want* him?"

"Of course we want him," said Evie.

"We want every one of those kids that shows up on our door."

"We want Ked even more."

"We want him special."

"Well, that's what I mean," I said. "He's wanted here. He should be able to stay where he is wanted."

"It don't work like that, honey," said Evie. "But I'll tell you what, if we ever got the option, we'd keep him. Like if he was offered to us."

"Of course we would," said Bert.

"Did I tell you, Primrose, that I got a recipe for baked potatoes with marshmallows? You know that people think they're just good with sweet potatoes but I figured a potato is a potato and I started to experiment."

"Evie's experimental recipes are the best. I keep telling her she should write a book," said Bert.

"I should, Bert, except I'd rather give the recipes to Ked and Primrose to use in *their* book. Now, come in the kitchen, Primrose, and stay for lunch and I'll show you."

But because Pooch seemed to demand many walks to keep him from ruining the trailer, we ended up not making the mini marshmallow baked potatoes until later that afternoon. They were ready for my dad and Ked when they got back from fishing. They both came into the trailer with bright eyes and red cheeks and I think anything would have tasted good to them after all that hard labor and sea air, but even so, potatoes with mini marshmallows tasted better than you might think. Evie didn't want to give me the recipe yet because she said she was still honing it, so I took her recipe for penuche instead.

Penuche with Mini Marshmallows

Combine two and a quarter cups of brown sugar with three quarters of a cup of milk and a pinch of salt in a saucepan. Stir over medium heat until it dissolves and then cook until it comes to the soft ball stage. You do this by dropping a bit in a glass of cold water and seeing if you can form a soft ball with it. It's a lot of fun to do but don't get so carried away that you use up half your mixture this way. You may think this sounds daft but it's kind of mesmerizing. Take it off the heat and add two and a half tablespoons of butter. Let it cool down. Stir in a teaspoon of vanilla. Stir it until it is thick and creamy and then add one cup of mini marshmallows and pour it into a buttered 9×5-inch pan. Let it cool even more and cut into pieces.

Vegetarian War Orphan Chili

Chop two onions and fry in some olive oil. Add a smattering of bay leaves, oregano, cumin, allspice, cinnamon, and cloves and a chunk of unsweetened chocolate. Chop up two stalks of celery, two green peppers, two jalapeños and two cloves of garlic and add them. Then add two cans of chopped green chilies, two packages of soy burger, three cans of tomatoes, one can of kidney beans, one can of black beans and one can of corn. Let it cook for a while. That's it.

What Happened to Ked

I SUFFERED A WHOLE week with Miss Lark before I decided that she was the person least fit to teach in the entire universe. She didn't even make a pretense of wanting us to learn. She shoveled assignments at us and then sat at her desk and worked on her latest manuscript. If you needed help she told you to go away and stop bothering her, she had cat poems to write. When she finished one she would try it out on us. Today's read,

> *The cat is our friend*
> *Of this I am sure*
> *They never have to teach*
> *Or other things endure*
> *Their lives are quite cushy*
> *Of that I can dream*

> *My pussies, you live with*
> *Your rear ends in cream*

Then she got mad when people snickered. But she kept reading us her poems anyway. She and Eleanor simply *loved* each other. By the end of the week I wanted to die.

I ran home after school Friday to get my bike and was surprised to see our car in the driveway. At first I was thrilled because I wanted to recite Miss Lark's latest poem to my mother but I didn't get the chance because the first thing she said to me was

"I was fired."

"Oh no. What did you do?" I asked.

"Well, I was laid off is maybe more accurate," she said. "Miss Clarice just said that things had changed and my services were no longer needed as of today. And it's my opinion that she's getting married. She had a big diamond ring on her finger."

"Who would want to marry her?" I asked.

"Clearly no one from around here. But I figure that diamond ring didn't just grow there. I thought it might be someone staying at the B and B, as obviously this all came up quite suddenly. There are two men who arrived this week that I think are possible candidates, even though they're both over sixty. Anyhow I asked if she had hired anyone else to replace me and she got very snippy and said no, she didn't think she would be needing anyone."

"Gosh," I said. "Maybe she is selling the B and B the way Uncle Jack predicted. But doesn't she have to give you two weeks' notice or something?"

"It's the other way around, Primrose. A little warning might have been nice. Not that it would make any difference. There aren't any other jobs in Coal Harbor that I know of anyway."

"What will you do?"

"I dunno. Think of something else." She sighed.

I felt bad leaving her like that but I'd promised Ked I would bring Mallomar over. Mallomar is a very discerning dog and I knew she wouldn't think much of this snapping, snarling playmate, and she didn't, but Ked kept insisting that his dog just needed socializing, so we took them to the beach, where Ked's dog got away and almost got hit by a car.

"He needs a name so you can call him back when he takes off like that. Otherwise, next time he might not be so lucky," I said.

But nothing we could think of seemed right.

Then I remembered to tell Ked about Miss Lark and her latest poem.

"She keeps reading them to us, even though kids snicker," I said. "And today Rachel came in from recess with her knee all bloody and was crying and Miss Lark didn't even ask her what happened. She barely looked up from her manuscript, just said, 'You know how to find the nurse's office.' She didn't even *care*."

"Well, I guess that's one way to avoid a nervous break-down," said Ked.

• • •

The next day Ked and I biked out to the end of Jackson Road to see if there was any logging activity yet. I always expected someday to be shocked to find trees falling. We were shocked, all right, but not by logging trucks. Instead right in front of the B and B property there was a huge FOR SALE sign.

"She's getting married and MOVING!" I said. "Miss Bowzer's dream can come true. No, wait, this is terrible. Uncle Jack is out of town. He has to buy the B and B before Dan Sneild does."

"I thought you'd decided your uncle doesn't love Miss Bowzer after all," said Ked.

"Well, she can't marry Dan Sneild. This is all wrong. Come on, let's go to The Girl on the Red Swing and see if Miss Bowzer knows about the B and B."

So we biked back to town and burst into the kitchen, where Miss Bowzer was making soup with her ragged little array of sous-chefs.

"I don't have room for anyone else in this kitchen, Primrose, sorry," she said while busily dodging people to do her usual six hundred things at once. "Here, have one of Verna's party cookies. She taught me how to make them this afternoon."

One of the vegetarian war orphans was now teaching *Miss Bowzer* things? I didn't like this. I didn't like this at all.

But it was such a good cookie that I got the recipe from Verna before continuing.

When I was done adding it to my notebook, I said, "I'm not here to help, Miss Bowzer. I'm here with *news*. The B and B is for sale!"

"Huh," she said. "Big news."

I didn't know what to say to this. But I didn't have to say anything because just then one of the vegetarian war orphans was coming across the kitchen with a huge industrial soup pot full of cut-up vegetables, didn't see me, tripped over my foot, and spilled the whole mess on the floor.

"Primrose, REALLY," snapped Miss Bowzer, as if it were my fault. "You and Ked are two bodies too many! Out! Out! Out!"

I had never been thrown out of Miss Bowzer's kitchen before. But Ked grabbed me and yanked me right out the door.

"Come on," he said. "Let's get Mallomar and Ruffian. They haven't had their playtime yet."

The day before, my dad had run into us on the beach with the dogs and had bent to pat Ked's dog, saying, "Who's this little ruffian?" And Ked had decided on the spot that Ruffian was the perfect name. Of course these days everything my dad did was perfect as far as Ked was concerned. Talk about hero worship.

We got our dogs and met back on the beach, where

Ruffian tried to slip his collar and kill Mallomar. I must say, Mallomar and I were extremely forbearing.

"Dan Sneild is going to buy the B and B and swoop up Miss Bowzer," I said in despair as we pulled Ruffian off Mallomar's throat.

"We don't really know what's going to happen," said Ked. "She doesn't seem that interested in the B and B anymore."

"We may not *know* what's going to happen, but we can *guess*," I said, refusing to be consoled. "I don't know how things could get worse."

But they did.

The next day I suffered through another day of cat poems. Miss Lark ended with

> *Pussy pussy on the hill*
> *Why so quiet, why so still?*
> *Why no movement for so long?*
> *Was it something I did wrong?*
> *Are you just a peaceful cat?*
> *Meditating this and that?*
> *On your tranquil grassy bed*
> *Oh, my goodness, you are dead!*

Eleanor cried at the end of this one and Miss Lark gave her extra credit for it.

I was relating all this despairingly to Ked after school

as we walked our bikes into town, but when we got there we could tell something was up. The one road leading into Coal Harbor from the east part of Vancouver Island was clogged with protesters and banners and people chanting and singing. All down the road were logging trucks, piled up and unable to get by.

"I guess they've started," said Ked.

"I thought Dan Sneild said he would give everyone fair warning before they started logging."

"Well, of course that's what he *said*," said Ked.

We got our bikes and headed out to Jackson Road. When we got as far as the B and B we could see more commotion there. Some of the loggers had apparently slipped in and started work before the protesters had had time to assemble. There was a stripe taken out of the mountain already. It was gray, ugly, stark.

A lot of townspeople were coming down the road to view the stripe. And there was the kind of grim quiet you get at a funeral.

It was silent on Jackson Road but it was no longer still. It turned out it wasn't the removal of the trees but the stillness I minded most. And it made me realize that stillness isn't because nothing is there. It is because so much is.

The next day the vegetarian war orphans posted a sign-up sheet at town hall for people volunteering to be arrested. They said it was important to have a steady flow of new people getting hauled off to jail. I still hadn't made my decision but I didn't seem to need to yet, as the first sign-up sheet for volunteers was full.

Some people were worried about who was going to run the town if everyone was sitting in jail, but it actually worked out pretty well. Nobody stayed in jail long. Everyone was getting bailed out. As time went by we got used to people going to jail and other people covering for them in their jobs. A lot of it happened while we were in school, but it was always interesting to see who was missing each day. My principal went to jail. Evie went to jail one day and Bert another. My mom went to jail. My dad was waiting for a day when it was too rough to go out in his boat. It got to be sort of routine. People would meet up and say, Yeah, I got some groceries, went to jail, picked up the kids at school . . . But, of course, as much as we made light of it, it was serious because everyone would now have this on their record.

The protest annoyed the loggers and slowed down the logging but even so, the trees kept coming down and the scar grew larger and sadder-looking.

Ked and I went to the protest every day to watch but hadn't seen the arrests yet because they happened mornings when we were in school. Ked didn't seem to care about this so much but I secretly wanted to see them before I made up my mind about whether or not I would let myself get arrested. The only day we could do this was Saturday.

"I don't want to miss a day of fishing," said Ked. He was going out every Saturday now because my dad said he was a huge help and a fast learner.

"You won't. My dad said he'd wait for you. If we get there by eight we can watch it and then you can go."

"I don't want to make your dad wait."

"He already said it was fine. That with your help on the boat he can afford to leave a bit later. He *wants* us to see the arrests. He says it's educational. And I don't want to go without you."

Ked rolled his eyes but he promised to watch the arrests before going fishing.

Then I felt bad for bullying him into it but not bad enough to say, Don't come.

We agreed to meet at the beginning of Jackson Road on Saturday morning but when I got there Ked was nowhere to be seen. It was already after eight. I could hear the protesters from way down the road, singing. I debated pushing on ahead, hoping Ked would figure things out and find me. I waited at the end of the road another ten minutes, and when he still hadn't come, it occurred to me that maybe he had changed his mind and gone straight down to the docks. Just in case he had been held up for some other reason, I waited yet another ten minutes. When he still hadn't shown up, I knew he wasn't coming so I biked on toward the protesters alone.

At the end of the road there was a huge crush of people. More than there ever was later in the day. Apparently everyone liked watching the arrests. The sheriff hadn't arrived yet so I looked for a good viewing point. I tried to peer over shoulders but I couldn't see anything over the sea of people. Some of the protesters had built little platforms in the trees farther back in the forest as the second line of defense for when the time came. If I could climb that high I would get a bird's-eye view. I walked my bike up the mountain to a platformed tree and managed to climb up just as the sheriff rolled around in his car. Ked was *really* going to be sorry he missed this, I thought. It felt historic and dramatic. Full of pomp and ceremony, the way a good parade is. Good parades always make me teary and I fogged up a bit as the sheriff strode from his car to the protesters, court injunction in hand. Everyone was so serious and full of suppressed emotion, which seemed to manifest in a strange stilted version of their normal selves.

The chief logger went up to the first girl chained to the log and asked her if she was going to move and she said, "No, sir, I'm sorry, sir, but I'm not." Her voice was shaking slightly, whether with the import of the moment or sudden fear, you couldn't tell. Then the sheriff showed her the court injunction and she said, "I'm sorry. I wish no violence but I cannot move from this spot. I break the law as a matter of conscience. These trees should remain for our children and our children's children."

Nobody was talking the way they usually did. There was a solemnity and formality to their language that was a little awkward and embarrassing but you could tell they felt their normal vernacular didn't fit the majesty of the occasion, the way no one talks normally in church but feels they have to hark back to an earlier, more grandiloquent era. I was surprised she didn't throw in some *thee*s and *thou*s.

Then the sheriff arrested her and put her in the car and moved on to the next protester. He got to one of the protesting grannies and asked her to move and she said, "No, sir, I'm sorry but I can't. I do this for your grandchildren and for mine. I have seen miles of ancient forest removed in my lifetime and have been to many futile protests. As far as I'm concerned this is now an emergency situation."

The poor sheriff looked as sad as she did when he handcuffed her. He could only haul two protesters away at a time so he had to make three trips to the jail and back. By the time he was done I was chilly and hungry. I decided to bike back to ask Bert and Evie if Ked had left a message for me, like, Sorry I was too much of a weasel to go to the arrests.

As I biked to the trailer park I got more and more irritated with him. If he hadn't planned to come he should have just said so in the first place. Or at least stopped off to tell me so on his way to the docks. But as soon as Bert opened the door I knew something was terribly wrong. Bert looked at me and at first he didn't say anything, as if he didn't even know who I was. I heard Evie crying in Ked's bedroom.

"What's the matter?" I asked. "What has happened?"

Bert hemmed and hawed and pulled at his face until Evie opened the bedroom door, asking, "Who is it?" through her sobs. When she saw me, she wiped her face and very quietly took me over to the couch.

"Honey, I got some bad news for you. But we got to think it's good news for Ked."

"*What?*" I said too sharply.

"His dad came," she said.

"And a social worker," said Bert.

"His *DAD*?" I said. "*WHAT* dad?"

"Well, he has a dad just like a lot of people. You know we don't get no big details about these things. We were told his dad was out—"

"Out of *WHERE*?" I interrupted.

"We don't know. It isn't our business. That's just what the social worker said, his dad was out and wanted to get Ked because he was taking off right away and Ked had to go with him."

"Taking him off to *where*?"

"We don't know. We kind of hoped someone would tell us, Ked even, but no one did. We don't know much of anything."

"But Ked didn't want to go, did he? Couldn't he tell the social worker he wanted to stay here? He's coming back, isn't he?"

"No, honey," said Bert. "These kids, they're just with us for a while. They're not permanent. We get them over a bad patch. Now his dad has got him back."

"His dad must ALWAYS be having bad patches because Ked's always getting put places. And he wants to stay here. He found a home here. He can *fish* here."

"Well, we don't know what he wanted. He didn't say much, Primrose. It wasn't up to him to begin with, and he must have had mixed feelings, and if it's a shock for you, think how it must have been for him, his dad just showing up so suddenlike," said Evie.

"Well, they did call first, Evie," said Bert. "Last night. To say they were coming. And I got a feeling it didn't surprise Ked much. He's used to it."

"But why didn't he call me and tell me?"

"Well, the social worker's call came kind of late."

"I expect it was all kind of upsetting for him too," said Evie. "I expect he just didn't know how to tell you."

"But he didn't even say GOODBYE!" I said.

"Some folks can't," said Evie.

"That's a fact," said Bert.

Then I heard a bark.

"He didn't take Ruffian?"

I ran into Ked's bedroom. Ruffian jumped on me and

then I saw the scrapbook Evie had been making Ked with the pictures of him on his first day fishing and its half-made macramé cover.

"No," said Bert, following me. "We offered, of course, when the dad and social worker were here but the dad didn't want no dog."

"Not everyone's a dog person," said Evie.

"No, they aren't," said Bert.

"But didn't Ked tell his dad that Ruffian was *his* dog?"

"He did. He did just ask his dad if he couldn't take Ruffian but the dad said no and that was that."

"His dad must be a MONSTER!" I said, and I began to cry. I didn't want to cry in front of Bert and Evie but I couldn't help it.

"We can't believe that, Primrose," said Evie.

"We can't afford to believe that," said Bert. "We can't stand to think that's so. Some people, well, they just don't understand dogs. They're not dog people. We gotta think he'll be good to Ked in other ways."

"Did Ked say anything like he'd call or write or did he leave a message for me?"

"To tell you the truth, Primrose, after we got the call saying they were coming to get him, he didn't say much of anything at all."

Verna's Party Cookies

Mix well with beaters one cup of butter, one cup of powdered sugar and two teaspoons of vanilla. Add to it and mix well one and a quarter cups of flour, half a teaspoon of salt and one cup of oatmeal. Drop from a spoon on an ungreased tin. Press half of a pecan on top of each one. Bake at 350 for twelve to fifteen minutes. Then whoop it up.

What Happened in the End

EVERYONE WAS ALMOST AS sad as I was that Ked had left. "I should have known he would have shown up unless something like that had happened," my dad kept saying over and over. He felt bad that he had pushed off with the idea that Ked had decided to be arrested instead of go fishing. "He was one of the best workers I ever saw. And the most conscientious. I should have known."

"But no one could have known," I said.

For a while I kept thinking that it was a mistake and I would find Ked returned to Bert and Evie. I wanted to go check every day after school in case he had shown up. But I didn't want Bert and Evie to figure out I was coming over hopefully. It would just rub things in. They were upset enough as it was. I knew I should visit them without

Ked being there but I just couldn't. I'd be listening for his footsteps constantly.

Then one day after school as I walked Mallomar on the beach, enjoying, to be truthful, not having to leash her for Ruffian's sake, I got to feeling guilty. Even if it was painful, I should at least go to the trailer long enough to pick up Ruffian and continue with Ked's program of socializing him by making him walk with Mallomar. I knew it was what Ked would want.

Every day after school I planned to bite the bullet and go see Bert and Evie and take Ruffian off their hands for an hour. And every day, halfway there I would turn around and go home instead.

I didn't watch the protests all week either. Everyone left me alone to mope, except for Eleanor, who rushed up to me at recess to tell me how awful the mountain was looking.

"The whole top is bare now," she said.

"Is that supposed to make me happy?" I asked.

"Miss Bowzer is getting arrested next," she said importantly.

"Impossible. She's on the side of the loggers. She wouldn't even sign the letter."

"Well, I guess she changed her mind. So now you're not the only one who gets to help out at The Girl on the Red Swing. My mom is going to help out and she said I could too."

That Eleanor would be working there and I didn't even know that Miss Bowzer needed help made me feel really cut off.

"Mr. and Mrs. Abruzzi are helping too," said Eleanor.

"Bert and Evie?" I said. I realized that even though Ked had left, the town was still functioning, with people helping each other while I had crept off to lick my wounds. So after school I charged over to see if they had made arrangements for someone to take Ruffian the day they'd be working at the restaurant. Evie said the people next door were watching him.

"We didn't want to ask you, honey," said Evie.

"Or your mom," said Bert.

"Because we knew you, well, needed a little time to get used to it."

"Have you heard from him or the social worker or anything?" I asked.

"Not from Ked, but the social worker said he and his dad arrived safely in Yellowknife."

"YELLOWKNIFE?" I cried. "That's the Northwest Territories!"

"Well, I guess it is," said Bert.

"It's FREEZING there. There's nothing but ice and snow and tundra. There are no fishing boats there."

"Now, I've known folks go up there and fall in love with the North. They got northern lights."

"And probably those beautiful polar bears. I've always

thought polar bears looked so mystical," said Evie. "He'll see lots of beautiful things he wouldn't have no chance to otherwise."

"He might love it there, Primrose," said Bert.

"He won't. And all he has is a thin little Windbreaker. And the rain jacket you bought him."

"Oh, I'm sure his dad has bought him a good warm coat by now," said Evie, but she didn't look sure at all. Her eyes got all big as if it had suddenly occurred to her too that Ked might be shivering even as we spoke.

I almost wished I didn't know where he had gone. That I could imagine him in some coastal village where he was warm enough and could fish.

"Well, now at least I can write him."

"Honey, we're not supposed to tell anyone about him without his wishes and he didn't leave no wishes. Besides, we don't have an address. He might not even be there still, his dad might be just staying there temporary."

"Well, he'll write to *us*, won't he?"

"We gotta hope he does because we got no way to contact him," said Evie.

"But, honey," said Bert, "if he don't, you can't take it personally. We've had a lot of these kids over the years and sometimes, you know, they get placed in a lot of different homes. I got the feeling Ked was and they can't all keep up all the time."

"But this was different," I said.

"I'm sure it was, honey," said Bert. "But you gotta know how hard it is for these kids. Sometimes it's easier for them to let go."

I took Ruffian and walked to the beach. I did a run down the sand with the two dogs. They pulled me so hard that I felt like they were my dogsled team and I imagined this brought me closer to Ked. I was sure Bert and Evie were wrong. I was sure I'd have a letter by the following week. If Ked wrote as soon as he got there, the letter should easily be with me Monday.

But it wasn't. Not Monday or Tuesday or Wednesday. Thursday Miss Bowzer was to be arrested. I stopped at The Girl on the Red Swing after school to see how Bert and Evie were getting on. The restaurant was full and everyone was enjoying the new menu, as of course Evie had put mini marshmallows in everything. The seer's eyes followed me the whole time. I noticed he was digging into Evie's special Polynesian Jell-O Salad, which was chockablock full of marshmallows. I think Evie put extras on his. Afterward, I picked up Mallomar and went to the trailer park to get Ruffian from Bert and Evie's neighbors and take him for his run.

I thought of Ked all alone and cold up north in some wasted landscape with maybe some father who was so awful he couldn't even tell me about him, and I ran harder and harder. For some reason this worked Ruffian into a frenzy and he began barking and leaping up on me and snapping until he bit my hand. I screamed. Then I threw down my end of the leash and shouted, "Just GO, then, if that's how you're going to be. Just GO!" I was suddenly sick of trying to care for this dog who didn't appreciate it and was bent on trying to kill himself.

Ruffian was off like a shot and I sighed and Mallomar and I ran after him. He was a full block ahead of us when an old souped-up convertible turned the corner. The car bore down on Ruffian and for a split second you could see Ruffian speed up. He was going to make it to the other side, I thought thankfully, and then the driver, who clearly didn't see him, sped up as well and there was a terrible bang and the car ran right over Ruffian and kept going. I don't think the driver even realized what he had done.

By the time I got to Ruffian, he was dead. He had probably died on impact. I sat down on the curb and everything that had gone wrong caught up with me. Ruffian and Ked had found a safe refuge for so short a time and now they were gone. All the snapping and snarling had gone out of Ruffian and he was lying there so vulnerably I couldn't bear it. I took my sweater off and put it on top of him so no one could see the vulnerable side of him he had been so careful to protect. Then I had to lie down right there on the pavement because I felt nauseated and faint. Mallomar lay down next to me, making soft whining noises. After a while she tried to lick me back into some normal state but I didn't think I would ever have a normal state again.

Suddenly there was a warm hand on my shoulder and I startled for one second, thinking it was Ked, as if he were reaching out ethereally for me. To tell you the truth, I can see how under stress people could lose their marbles.

"Primrose?"

I looked up and was so distraught that I wasn't even particularly surprised to see Uncle Jack, who had been gone for weeks.

"I just got back into town. I stopped at The Girl on the Red Swing and they told me Kate was in jail so I was just going down there to make sure she had been bailed out," he said. "What's under the sweater?"

"Ruffian. Ked's dog. A car hit him. Ked doesn't even know. His dad took him to Yellowknife," I said.

Uncle Jack nodded. "Yeah, Evie told me about Ked. They should have put a stop sign there a long time ago," he said angrily. "Come on, Primrose, I'll take you home, then I'll come back and deal with it."

"I don't want to go home."

"Where are your mom and dad?"

"Dad's fishing and Mom's at the protest."

"Right," said Uncle Jack. "Let's take Mallomar home and then take care of everything else."

After we took Mallomar back, I walked with Uncle

Jack to his office and we got a garbage bag and a box for Ruffian. We decided to take him to Uncle Jack's office and then tell Bert and Evie what had happened and see what they wanted done with the body. After we dropped Ruffian's body at Uncle Jack's, we headed over to The Girl on the Red Swing, and I thought that all they needed was more unexpected sadness. On the way over I kept trying to think how best to break it to them, wondering if they would blame me for not keeping a tighter hold on Ruffian, but when I finally blurted it out, they just hugged me.

"It's not your fault, Primrose. There was nothing anyone could do with that dog when he got that way. He was always a wild dog. And now at least they'll put a stop sign on that corner," said Evie.

"Not that it's any consolation," said Bert.

"And, Primrose, you know Ked wouldn't blame you neither," said Evie. "He'd know you were just as broken-hearted about it as he was."

Uncle Jack seemed to sense that I couldn't talk, and we walked over to the jail without saying much. When we got there we found out my mom had already bailed out Miss Bowzer earlier in the day.

"Where would she go then?" I said.

"Maybe she's protesting with your mom," said Uncle Jack.

So because I still didn't want to go home and neither did Uncle Jack we decided to head out that way.

When we got to the end of Jackson Road we found my mother. She said Miss Bowzer had been drifting about but she hadn't seen her lately. Uncle Jack and I strolled on, looking for her. It was noisy, between the sounds of chain saws and falling limbs and the singing and chanting. I was so rattled and vibrating already that it was giving me a terrible headache. The whole top of the mountain was bare.

We finally found Miss Bowzer sitting on the top steps of the B and B. All Miss Clarice's furniture had been moved down island, even the porch furniture. Miss Bowzer was staring at the mountain glumly. When she saw Uncle Jack, her eyes lit up momentarily, and then she turned her gaze back to the mountain.

"You look as miserable as Primrose," said Uncle Jack, clearly floundering the way he always did around Miss Bowzer. He and I plunked ourselves down on the step next to her. My headache was getting worse and worse, so that it seemed to be vibrating as much as the chain saws.

"Of course she's miserable," said Miss Bowzer tartly. "Because Ked is gone. Everybody's who's been *around* knows that."

"Ruffian was just killed by a car," said Uncle Jack quietly. "She *saw* it happen."

"Oh, you poor thing," said Miss Bowzer. "What an awful thing to witness."

They both looked at me sympathetically but not really

understanding at all, and it detonated all the stuff inside I had felt but not told anyone.

"I DIDN'T *SEE* IT HAPPEN! I CAUSED IT! I KILLED KED'S DOG! HE BIT ME SO I TURNED HIM LOOSE AND TOLD HIM TO GO PLAY IN TRAFFIC AND HE *DID*!"

Uncle Jack squinted as he sized me and the situation up and then he said quietly, "Don't be silly. You didn't think that would happen. It wasn't deliberate."

"AND I DIDN'T SAVE KED!" I said in new agony because this was the thing that had really been bothering me for some time.

"No, but you don't know how things will turn out for him. Just because he's out of our hands doesn't mean nothing good will ever happen to him. It's certainly his turn," said Uncle Jack.

"I thought you didn't believe in justice," I said in surprise.

"I don't but I believe in the occasional miracle. If I didn't I wouldn't be asking . . . ," and he was opening his sports jacket when I remembered something else.

"AND I NEVER TOLD HIM HE WAS MY BEST FRIEND! I NEVER *TOLD* HIM! AND NOW HE'LL NEVER KNOW!"

Miss Bowzer, who had been looking concerned for me and irritated with Uncle Jack, frowned, looked a million miles away, and suddenly shot up, yelling, "I WANT TO

GET MARRIED! I WANT TO GET MARRIED. I
WANT *YOU* TO MARRY ME!"

Poor Uncle Jack looked stunned. Women were leaping
around porch steps shouting unexpected things with no
apparent provocation.

After a pause to take in this new information, he said
quietly, "Okay. Okay, I'll marry you."

"I DON'T WANT TO *MAKE* YOU MARRY ME! I
DON'T WANT IT TO BE *MY* IDEA!"

Uncle Jack stood up, mopped his brow and took Miss
Bowzer by the shoulders and whirled her to face him. He
had beads of sweat all over his upper lip, and his hair was
kind of standing on end. "That's not what I . . . If you'll
just hold still one second, you'll see I'm trying to declare
myself."

"Oh!" said Miss Bowzer, and all the air went out of
her and she collapsed onto the steps with an audible
whomp.

"Jeez, *Louise!*" said Uncle Jack. He opened his sports
jacket again and from an inside pocket took out a small
box and handed it to her. "What I was about to say before
I was interrupted was that if I didn't believe in the occasional miracle I'd never have the nerve to ask you to be
my wife. I've been carrying this around for months."

Miss Bowzer opened the box. Inside was a beautiful,
sparkling ring. There was an emerald in the middle that I
bet he got because it was the color of Miss Bowzer's eyes.

Good ring choice, I wanted to say, until I remembered that this was supposed to be a romantic moment and not a jewelry critique.

"Do you suppose you could excuse us for a minute?" Uncle Jack asked, looking down at me. I realized what I must look like, staring up at them with my mouth open, my face all blotchy, practically drooling on the bottom step. I was hardly adding anything decorative to the occasion so I moved off.

I walked among the protesters but looked back at the porch steps from time to time to try to catch a glimpse of the big romantic moment, but Uncle Jack and Miss Bowzer had gone around the side of the house to have it alone.

They were gone so long I had time to replay everything that had happened in one year in Coal Harbor. As I did, my temples slowly stopped throbbing and my headache began to dissipate. For a small town an awful lot had gone on. A lot of it had been sad and now some of it was my fault. But at least, finally, something really happy had happened.

Miss Bowzer and Uncle Jack were returning to the porch and there was a point I was suddenly curious about.

I ran over. I noticed that the ring was now on Miss Bowzer's finger.

"Why did you wait so long?" I asked Uncle Jack. "If you already had the ring?"

"I wanted to have things worked out first," said Uncle Jack.

This was so like him. He always wanted all the pieces in his deals put together perfectly and all the angles figured out before he acted on them.

"I wanted us to have something we could do together, Kate, or at least in proximity," he said, turning to her. "At first I thought I'd get a successful restaurant going and then we could have two restaurants. I thought you'd *like* that. I certainly didn't want to continue working down island so much after we were married, that is if you decided to accept me."

"Oh, you!" she said, smiling and nudging him in the ribs with her elbow, which put her diamond-clad hand at a particularly good display angle. I imagined we were going to see the hand at that angle quite a bit in the weeks to come. And why not? Miss Bowzer had waited a long time for someone who would go out into the storm after her, forsaking all else.

"Then when I realized you wanted the B and B—"

"When I *told* you she did," I interjected.

"Right, when Primrose told me you did, then I decided to sell a bunch of my holdings down island and buy it. Dan and Miss Clarice, soon to be Mrs. Sneild, had asked me to find them a farm down island to transfer her buffalo enterprise, so I was busy with that as well."

"Dan Sneild is marrying Miss Clarice?" I interrupted. "Oh, the snake! He was courting Miss Bowzer!"

"Oh, hush, Primrose, I knew about Miss Clarice all along," said Miss Bowzer. "Dan followed her up here from Duncan and told me the first night that he was going to try to convince her to move back with him."

"Well, you certainly had *me* fooled," I sniffed.

"Hush," said Miss Bowzer again. "I want to hear what Jack has to say."

"Oh," said Uncle Jack. "Well, I figured once I had the B and B secured, I would ask you to marry me. I was going to put an offer on it today, actually. Miss Clarice knew I'd be making one as soon as I could. But now, looking at that clear-cut, I'm worried about this B and B doing business. Maybe we should look for another with a better view."

"No," said Miss Bowzer stubbornly. "I want this one. I've always wanted this one."

We all stared at the big ugly bald strip across the way.

"All right then," said Uncle Jack dubiously. "But hey! Here's a happy thought—we can serve all the French food we want!"

"Oh! So that's what that was about? You were *auditioning* me?" And Miss Bowzer started to turn an irritated scarlet, proving that she could get prickly even at the most romantic of moments. I could tell they were going to have some spectacular dustups in the years to come.

I decided to change the subject before the French food could be further explored and my own nefarious part in the *boeuf bourguignon* affair be revealed.

"It's too bad you can't buy the *mountain*," I said hastily. "That would stop the logging."

And that's when Uncle Jack stood up and left. Without a word.

"NOW WHAT!" said Miss Bowzer, to no one in particular. "NOW WHERE DID HE GO?"

She was still shouting everything as if she weren't aware she had a volume control.

"Don't worry," I said. "I know that look on Uncle Jack's face. He didn't just disappear. He has a plan."

• • •

That's how Mendolay Mountain ended up with a statue of Mr. Honeycut on top of it. The strip that had been clear-cut was planted in wildflowers and kept tidy by the Honeycut Park Preservation Committee. Even though there was a lot of grumbling about it, I was kind of glad Miss Honeycut got a statue of her father up there. Although he was a pretty scary-looking guy. You'd think they'd at least have made the statue smile but instead they gave him a frown and a huge nose down which he could look at all of us forever. Which maybe Miss Honeycut would have liked, I don't know. She never came to see it. We invited her for the dedication ceremony but I think she was at someone or other's dying bedside and just wrote a letter to be read, saying a mountaintop park had exceeded her expectations and how clever Uncle Jack was. This part made everyone snicker.

I thought the vegetarian war orphans would be ecstatic that the logging had stopped but they looked a little bemused, as if they'd had their protesting carpet yanked out from underneath them, all dressed up in placards and no place to go. But in the end they graciously forgave Uncle Jack for this and headed to their next protest, on the mainland. All except for the one who had once been a hairdresser. He decided to stay in town.

After that, Uncle Jack took off for the Alberta oil fields, where men could make a lot of money fast if they were lucky. He had hoped to get money for the mountain from the land conservancy but even with that and Miss Honeycut's Coal Harbor fund, he had to put all the money he had planned to spend on the B and B into buying the mountain. So he had to start all over to make his fortune. And he had to do it quickly before someone else got the B and B. And it was just like Uncle Jack that he didn't make a fuss or promises or complaints. He just took off to do what he had to do. So that was that. Indefinitely.

"I'm an idiot," Miss Bowzer was saying to me and my mother as we sat around our kitchen table and admired her ring for the millionth time.

"Because you tried to make him jealous by pretending to care for Dan Sneild?" I asked. I had been curious on this point for some time.

"Primrose," said my mother warningly.

"No," said Miss Bowzer shortly.

I still thought that that had some choice idiot qualities about it, but if she wasn't willing to discuss it, there was no point in pursuing it.

"No, because he offers me the B and B I have always wanted, gives me a ring and I send him off to buy a mountain instead."

"It wasn't quite like that," I said. "You didn't really send him off. I was the one who suggested buying the mountain but it didn't occur to me that was actually possible. And besides, he's going to make it all work. That's what he does best."

"And what good would the B and B be if you sat on that porch and looked at that clear-cut? No, you did the right thing," said my mother, and sighed. "Old hotfoot Jack."

"He just wants to give you what you've always wanted," I said. "It's very romantic, really."

Miss Bowzer just shook her head. "Ha! Don't kid yourself. He's having a wonderful time. There's nothing he likes better than losing all his money and having to make it again. Part of me thinks he bought that mountain just so he'd have the thrill of having to start at square one."

I wanted to protest but I suspected she was probably right.

"No," she went on, "he just went whistling off. Well, who knows if he'll ever make enough money for the B and B? Who knows how many years we'll waste apart while he tries? Who knows if he'll ever come back? That man is going to drive me crazy."

• • •

With all the excitement and fuss in town over, and everyone returned to their normal routines, I had time to brood more about Ked. He was always on my mind. It made me kind of angry that everyone else seemed to have accepted that he was gone and that was that. I wondered if my parents would be willing to take a family trip to Yellowknife in the summer. I was asking my mom about this after supper one night when my dad flipped on the news.

"HUSH!" he said to my mother and me, which was so unlike him that we froze.

Then we heard what he did. The tail end of a story out of Yellowknife.

A reporter was saying, ". . . since a fourteen-year-old boy has disappeared off a frozen lake outside Yellowknife. His father, Jack Schneider—"

"That's Ked's last name!" I said.

"HUSH!" said my dad again as he strained to hear. My mother and I sat on the couch next to him.

"RCMP officers say that the father claims to have forgotten his tackle and left the boy alone on the ice while he drove back for it. A bartender says Mr. Schneider arrived at his bar and began drinking, at one point got agitated, seeming to suddenly remember that he'd left his son out on the ice waiting for him. The bartender became concerned and called a local constable, who drove out to the lake and found footprints but no other signs of life. Search and Rescue has been called out but so far there is no sign of the boy."

My dad drove over to tell Bert and Evie in case they

hadn't already heard, while my mom and I sat in the living room glued to the television, but there was no more news.

My mom let me stay home from school the next day. I watched the news and took hot baths but I could not get warm and nothing more was reported.

"Do you think he found shelter?" I asked my mom when Search and Rescue was called off. "Just because they didn't find him doesn't mean he isn't alive."

"That's right," said my mom. But I knew she'd heard what I had, that it was thirty below.

Evie and Bert looked as haunted as I felt. We didn't talk about it. The first week we all hoped to hear something, anything indicating that Ked was all right. And as time went on, any other kind of speculation seemed unthinkable. Finally the only way I could cope was not to think about it at all. But it existed like a fifth appendage that hung on my body, throwing me off balance.

Miss Bowzer sensed I didn't want to talk about it but she kept saying she had faith in Uncle Jack coming back soon, and I thought half the time she was really talking about Ked. She must have had some faith in Uncle Jack making the money he said he would, too, because when she and I walked out to the end of Jackson Road, as we did from time to time, to sit on the B and B steps and gaze at Miss Honeycut's park, Miss Bowzer would tell me in detail how she saw each of the rooms decorated.

"He thinks he needs something to offer me before he can marry me," said Miss Bowzer. "It's stupid but you can't do much about people's built-in stupidity. I mean everyone's stupid in *some* form. I always thought that poor boy Ked was so quiet and shy because he thought he had nothing to offer anyone."

"I don't want to talk about it," I said stonily as I always did when someone brought him up.

We stared at the mountaintop with its ridiculous barely-able-to-be-seen statue perched high on top.

"Maybe you'll see Ked again someday. Maybe I'll see Jack. Life takes a lot of courage, Primrose. You can candy-coat that idea all you like but that's the truth. A lot of it's just hard."

"I don't want to talk about it. Sometimes it helps to pretend he was never here."

"Of course Ked was here," said Miss Bowzer, and I couldn't tell if she was intentionally misunderstanding me or not, but she seemed determined to keep resurrecting him with talk. "He was getting to be quite a fixture, coming into the restaurant every day. I really liked him, even though he hardly said a word."

"He didn't go to the restaurant every day. I was with him every day after school," I said.

"He came while he was waiting for your school to let out. I'd've thought he'd told you. At first I thought he was just killing time; then I realized he came in to pump the seer. He bought Harry something to eat every single day—a piece of pie or at least a cup of coffee or Coke or something. But he never bought himself nothing. I wanted to give him his own piece of pie for free, because he was always watching the seer eat it like he could put away half a pie himself. You know teenage boys. But the first time I offered he looked so embarrassed I didn't do that again. You know, I think he just didn't feel like he could show up and ask the seer to tell his dreamtown visions for free."

"But Ked never had any money," I said. "It was one of his chief complaints. That's why we were making the cookbook."

Then a thought struck me.

"How did he pay for the meals?"

"Cash," said Miss Bowzer, looking surprised.

"No, I mean bills or change?"

"Oh." She thought a second. "It was always change. Loonies, toonies, once he tried to pay for coffee all with pennies and I told him not to do that again. I don't need a hundred pennies."

"What did he ask the seer?" I said, putting my head in my hands. Eleanor had been right and Uncle Jack must have known it. But I didn't care. It didn't change my opinion of any of them.

"Well, gosh, let me think," Miss Bowzer said. "What did he ask the seer? I think Ked wanted to know what was going to happen to him next. Seems that when I did overhear Ked that's what he was asking about. But you know no one can tell you what's coming down the chute. Just as well."

• • •

Uncle Jack made his way back the following spring with a bank account full of money, just as he'd planned. Miss Bowzer sold The Girl on the Red Swing to Bert and Evie. Bert and Evie came over one night to tell us excitedly all about it.

"It was when we were helping Miss Bowzer run it that we got the bug," said Evie.

"The restaurant bug," said Bert.

"And we need something to do. Macramé is nice but it don't take up all your hours."

"And Evie loves feeding people."

"We got lots of ideas."

"Not that we'd change much really. We'd still serve everything on a waffle. But Evie's got some new recipes."

"With mini marshmallows," said Evie happily.

"But not everything with mini marshmallows," said Bert.

"Because some folks don't like them," Evie said to me in amazement. "They don't even like having to pick them out."

"And we want people to be happy there," said Bert.

"At least as happy as they were when Miss Bowzer ran it."

Nobody could have been as happy these days as Miss Bowzer unless it was Uncle Jack. We had the wedding for them in our backyard and Miss Bowzer, whom I was now supposed to call Kate, looked so beautiful I thought there could never be a more glowing bride. My mom and I got to help her make her dress, which was a lovely ivory simple thing. I don't know what she reminded me of, a mermaid or an angel or something. I swear she had a little golden aura around her all through the ceremony and for the rest of the day. I asked my mom if she could see it and she said she could. Evie made the wedding cake, which of course was chock-full of mini marshmallows. Uncle Jack said it was his favorite kind, although as far as I knew neither he nor anyone else had ever tasted such a concoction. But it was such a day that if things there weren't already your favorite, forevermore they would be.

I was happy the day of the wedding, you couldn't not be, we all were, glowing and golden and shining with it. And as usual I included Ked there, as if I carried him to events in my thoughts the way I used to drag my teddy bear along.

After the wedding when everyone had gone and my mother and I were sitting together in the garden sharing one last piece of cake, I mentioned all this to her. That I brought him places in my mind. That he should have been here eating cake too. That some fates seemed so unfair, right from the start, and then, as for Ked, all the way through.

"I hesitate to say this because I don't think it's something you understand until you're much older," said my mother, pausing and reconsidering, "if you understand it then. It's something my mother said to me and I didn't understand it, but now, as I get older, I begin to get inklings of what she meant. You know she died when I was sixteen, don't you?"

"From breast cancer," I said. My mom didn't talk about it much. Her mother died and left my mother with a younger sister and two younger brothers. My mother left home right after to find her stepfather, who had disappeared three years before. The older I got the more horrible my mother's teenage years sounded, although she always claimed they weren't horrible at all, just eventful. Only her mother dying was really terrible, she said.

"Well, when she was dying I kept saying it wasn't fair. She was such a wonderful person, everyone loved my mother. Well, most people did. She was such a beautiful poet and there was always a kind of awareness of the intrinsic sacredness in everything when you were with her. And it didn't seem right that some of the people I thought were horrible and who hadn't my mother's great love of life were perfectly healthy and here she was dying from something dreadful. And she said that she had come round to see that everyone's fates were beautiful. Even the ones that seemed most horrifying. That you had to be careful who you said this to because most people didn't understand and if you said you thought some child dying had a beautiful fate, well, they thought you were crazy or some kind of a monster. But she said she could see it now. Even her fate had a kind of luminous beauty to it.

Peculiarly and absolutely her own. That what we give back to life is our own unique experience of it. And I was angry because I didn't want her to die and I didn't want her to see leaving us kids as beautiful. But now as I get older and see a bigger picture, well, I think she was right. Maybe someday you'll see that."

Or maybe not, I thought bitterly, but I didn't say it out loud because I knew she was only trying to help.

"Well, anyway," she said. "Did you see the new room Kate decorated? She's got the living room finished too."

"Yeah," I said. "I was there last week."

"When I was there yesterday," my mother went on, "Jack was taking down all the platforms. The vegetarian war orphans didn't do much of a cleanup when they left. He said it was the last touch in returning the forest to how it was before the logging. They've planted trees in a lot of the bare places. . . ."

My mother droned on but I stopped listening when she said platform. I'd been so shell-shocked by the loss of Ked that I had forgotten the seer's message to me the first time Ked met him. That I would be alone on a platform and it would be important. To be honest, I thought it was just the ravings of a disturbed mind. But I *had* been alone on a platform. That was where I was when they took Ked away.

I thought about this for days and the more I thought about it, the more it disturbed me. I could think of no explanation for how the seer could have known about the platform. The only thing I could come up with was that he *could* see things. And then I wondered, If this was true, then was his dreamtown real? And could he see Ked now? Did he know where Ked was and if he was okay? I wanted to know but I was afraid. I was still afraid of the seer and afraid he might not see the truth but tell me something totally false, which I would then believe. Or what if he *could* see things but saw something that was worse than not knowing at all? So for a long time I put off going to The Girl on the Red Swing to talk to him.

But one night I lay awake all night and was so tired during school the next day that I couldn't think straight so I gave up and went over to The Girl on the Red Swing. Bert generally waited tables and Evie cooked. They both came over to say hello and beam at me but they looked a little nervous when I said I'd come to talk to the seer.

"Do you want me to join you, honey?" asked Bert, even though all the tables were filled and the place was hopping.

"No, it's kind of private," I said.

"Well, okay. I'll bring you a milk shake, shall I?"

"No, it's okay. I want to pay for the seer's lunch, though, because I need to ask him some questions. I've got the money right here." I handed it to him.

Bert looked unhappy about the whole thing. As I stood by the booth he explained to the seer that his lunch was on me and the seer immediately ordered liver and onions.

For a moment I had my doubts about him again. Anyone with extra powers should know that something like liver and onions is not going to go well on a waffle.

I slid into the booth across from the seer, who didn't seem surprised but looked at me blankly for a bit. I thought maybe he'd start the ball rolling by telling me things but he just put some more cream in his coffee and stirred it so slowly and contemplatively that for a second I wondered if that was where he saw his visions.

Finally, when it was apparent he wasn't going to say anything and maybe wasn't even quite aware of my presence, I said, "I guess you know Ked has been gone awhile."

He continued to look at me blankly.

"You remember Ked?" I said, prompting him.

The seer shook his head no and I wanted to shriek, Well, do you remember all the *MEALS* he paid for? Then I figured maybe Ked had never told him his name so I described Ked to him. That didn't seem to have any effect either and I was beginning to think I had been wrong and his ability to see visions was nonsense, as everyone had tried to tell me.

But I tried again. "I thought maybe you'd seen him lately in your dreams."

Now I really felt stupid and desperate but the seer seemed to come awake at the mention of his dreams.

"I see everything in my dreams. I see it all in my dreams. I see that boy you describe. Tall, hair over his eyes."

"Uh-huh," I said. And I thought about the first time I

saw Ked and how vulnerable he looked and I felt sad again.

"I see him. On a big expanse, lots of snow. Snow and ice. Cold. Blue. Northern lights."

The Northwest Territories, I thought excitedly, he *can* see him. And then I realized that this described pretty much all of Canada.

"I see him. I see him," said the seer, giving his coffee another stir.

"And is he okay?"

"Sure he is."

"Does he seem happy? Does he have a friend? Is he alone?"

The seer took a few minutes longer to answer, as if he were seeing it all as we talked.

"He's got animals with him. A dog. NO, *two* dogs. One small, fluffy. A cockapoo. One kind of wild. They go everywhere with him. They're looking out for him. He can't see them but they stay with him night and day."

"Jesus Christ!" I exclaimed, starting to cry and standing up. "No wonder Ked liked talking to you."

I wanted to leave but Evie, who was standing in the doorway watching me, bustled over and made me sit in the kitchen until I could calm down.

I didn't want to fall apart and start sobbing but I couldn't fight back the tears completely and a few made their way down my nose. Evie silently handed me a paper towel. I told her what the seer had said.

"Do you think he's crazy? I hope he's not just crazy," I said.

Evie sat down on a stool and looked sober and older than any time I'd seen her. "I don't know what to tell you, honey. On the odd days I think it takes more courage to think such things are crazy and on the even days I think it takes more courage to think they're not."

She gave me a glass of milk and a cookie but I wasn't hungry so I drank the milk and took the cookie with me as I slipped out the back kitchen door.

I didn't really know where to go after that. I finally ended up on Jackson Road, walking without thinking, feeling chilled and sleepless and stunned.

I walked until I came to the B and B. Kate was knitting on the porch.

"What's wrong?" she said, not lifting her eyes from her work.

So I told her what the seer had said and how I didn't know what to believe. "I think Evie was right," I said finally when Kate said nothing. "It can be a cruel world for the gentle creatures. You think you can take care of the ones within your reach but I don't know what to do for the ones who get cancer or taken away, or almost but don't quite make it across the street."

Kate said nothing and kept knitting and then I noticed that what she was knitting was booties. And we rocked and rocked the rest of the afternoon.

Evie Finally Perfects Her
Potato Marshmallow Recipe

She certainly slipped it in under the wire but here it is. Bake a potato until done, then slice it open. Take out the white part and mash with a tablespoon of butter, some salt and pepper, half a teaspoon of cinnamon and eight mini marshmallows. Return the mashed whites to the potato skins and place back in a 400-degree oven for fifteen minutes.

It was the exact number of mini marshmallows that had her stymied. Cooking seems easy until you come up against a problem like this.

But Then Something Else Happened

ALMOST A YEAR TO the day after I had first met Ked, Evie and Bert got a scare. In the middle of the night, someone pounded on their door.

"At first we thought it was a ghost," said Evie when they called to tell me.

But it was Ked.

My mom let me take the day off school and I went over to be with him. He was exhausted and stayed in bed telling Evie and me his strange story of stumbling through the forest after he realized his father wasn't returning to the lake with the fishing tackle, and shivering and knowing he might die of exposure and being found by an Inuit on a snowmobile and living with the Inuits' community, explaining to them he had no home. Finally, he said, he knew he couldn't stay on—although they'd been kind and let him live there, no questions asked. He hated the cold and snow so he decided to go south again but he was afraid the RCMP would get him and just deliver him back to his father. I guessed his father getting drunk and *forgetting* him on the ice, where he might have died, had been the last straw. The Inuit took him by snowmobile to the highway and he hitchhiked with truckers to Vancouver. He tried to live on the Vancouver streets for a while but he couldn't do it. So he came here.

"I have to tell the sheriff," said Evie when he was done.

"What's going to happen?" asked Ked.

"I don't know," said Evie.

"I can't go back there," he said.

"No, of course not," said Evie worriedly.

By evening Ked was well enough to eat at The Girl on the Red Swing. Kate had told me that she and Uncle Jack were planning to announce Kate's pregnancy that night, so the evening should have been very festive, but no matter how much we wanted to celebrate that and Ked's miraculous return, no one could help thinking of all that had happened to him in the meantime. Nevertheless, we were having pie, six kinds, all with mini marshmallows— Evie had dyed them pink and blue—when the sheriff walked in. With him were an RCMP officer, a social worker and someone who could only have been Ked's dad, even though he didn't look like Ked at all. He was a short, scruffy, squirrelly-looking guy, and every ounce of skin he had showing seemed to be covered in tattoos. His eyes were narrow and he didn't even *greet* Ked, just shuffled into a booth next to the social worker and looked sullen. There was complete silence as all of us except for Ked stared at him. I had a bite of pie almost to my mouth and I just sat stupidly holding it there. The social worker came over and took Ked to their booth, where they seemed to be questioning him and then his dad. This went on and on but they were speaking in such low voices that no one could hear what they were saying until suddenly Ked started to yell.

"No!" he yelled. "No way!"

I realized that in all the time I'd known him I'd never before seen him angry.

His dad began to yell too. "You should see what it's like to live with him. He steals, you know. He stole all the money I put under my mattress. That's why I had to leave him out on the ice."

"Wait a second," said the RCMP officer. "You left him there *on purpose?*"

"He's got to learn. He's always been uncontrollable. When he was little I used to have to tie him to the radiator. It was the only way. It's been a hard row to hoe being his father. He's been taking my money for years."

"Because we don't have food! We never have food. You don't care because you're always high!" yelled Ked.

"You tied him to radiators?" said the social worker,

who looked like she was suddenly in way over her head, unlike the RCMP officer, who looked weary, as if he wasn't hearing anything he hadn't heard a hundred times before.

The social worker's mouth opened and closed a few times before she finally came up with "Mr. Schneider, those are not good parenting skills."

I think all of us were feeling a little sick and then I felt I was floating above, watching, while Ked started to let loose. He was yelling things that would have had Eleanor's mom covering my ears. But through this I saw something else strange; it was as if Ked's anger were a ladder and with it he climbed down, down, down from the thin places. As if his anger were an affirmation that he was here too.

"I won't live with you," yelled Ked. "I'm done!"

"You got no choice, boy, and neither do I. They're gonna make me take you. I'm the only family you got. Who else would *want* you?" said his father.

Uncle Jack stood up. "I would," he said.

Kate, whose hands had been on her belly throughout this, like she was covering the unborn baby's ears, stood too. "We would."

Then my dad stood up. This meant sliding out of the booth. "I would too."

My mother looked bemused for a moment, as it probably occurred to her that we only had two small bedrooms, but she stood too and said, "Yes, he's ours."

"No, he's ours," said Evie, and she ran on her little legs and pulled Ked out of the booth to his feet and wrapped her arms around him, her face in his solar plexus.

"Darn right," said Bert.

"I would," a low rumbling voice came quietly from the back of the restaurant, and the seer stood up on his unsteady arthritic old legs. "If I wasn't so old, I would."

"Well, Ked," said the social worker, getting all business-like again and shuffling her papers. "We need to make some good choices now, don't we?"

• • •

Of course, it wasn't all smooth sailing from there. Ked's dad was arrested for failing to provide the necessities. Ked had to testify, which was pretty awful. He was, of course, going to live with Evie and Bert, who would start adoption procedures and were the ones to sit with him through his father's trial.

Having opened the tap to his anger and come down from the thin places, he wasn't sweet and spacy all the time anymore. He was grumpy some days and angry a lot of the time. He got in fights sometimes at school. He told me he didn't like cooking—that he had grown up cooking and caring for his dad and was sick of it. He still helped me with the cookbook, though. Bert encouraged him to join the ice hockey team at school. He seemed to enjoy it and I went to his games but I noticed he didn't talk much to anyone there. He told Evie he didn't like mini marshmallows but she didn't care. She started using chocolate chips instead and brought cookies to all his games and always proudly pointed out to everyone how fierce he was on the ice.

After a bit, some of the anger dropped away. It was almost as if after he found it, for a time it was the new toy. But when it started to go away he seemed a little lost.

He was predictably pretty upset about Ruffian. Evie and Bert found a litter of cockapoos in Kelowna and she and Bert and Ked all drove there to bring one home. Ked named him Gretzky. We got into the habit of walking Gretzky and Mallomar together when he didn't have hockey practice but Gretzky seemed more Evie and Bert's dog than Ked's.

One day he asked me to tell him about the accident. So I told him everything, even my fit of pique.

"I know you never liked Ruffian much, but you didn't send him deliberately to his death," said Ked.

"That's what Uncle Jack told me," I said.

"*You* just had a temper tantrum. *I* chose to live with people who said they wanted me rather than someone who didn't. Knowing that without me around to call 911, my dad is going to OD."

"You couldn't keep living there. He tried to kill you."

"Well, he didn't strangle me or shoot me. Leaving me on the ice, he probably thought I had a fifty-fifty chance." Ked smiled wryly.

"You made the right choice," I said. "And people didn't just say they want you, they really do."

But Ked just shook his head.

He still thinks he's a nuisance, I thought. All those years of being told he was, he can't quite believe otherwise. I wished for something so big that he had to believe people thought he had something to offer. Something that made him accept that he had a right to plant his feet here too. I didn't know what such a thing could be but I thought somewhere in this town, someone should be able to pull a rabbit out of a hat for him. I wanted to be like Uncle Jack and believe not in justice but in the occasional miracle but I didn't know what I believed in anymore.

Ked still fished every Saturday with my dad and had dinner with us every Saturday night. And he still bought the seer lunch every Sunday at The Girl on the Red Swing because he got to be so good at fishing that my dad started to pay him.

We sent *Just Throw Some Melted Butter on It and Call It a Day* to a publisher and they rejected it with a form letter so we never even found out what they didn't like about it. Miss Lark's book of cat poems, wittily titled *Cat Poems,* was published. One of Eleanor's cat pictures was chosen to illustrate the poem about the dead cat. She drew it lying on its back with all four paws in the air. It was supposed to be touching but it was just ridiculous. Plus she got her *name* in the book. And it turned out she even got *paid.* I tried to stir Ked up about this but he didn't seem to mind so much. He was listless a lot lately.

I thought about what my mother had said when Miss

Connon had her nervous breakdown. A person can be depleted.

I asked my dad what Ked was like on Saturdays when they were fishing but he said he seemed much the same as always.

And things moved on, of course, in Coal Harbor.

Miss Connon got better and came back to school. Her cousin stayed on in Coal Harbor because she had come to like living here. She was a hairdresser.

The granny from the protest meeting bought Uncle Jack's unfinished restaurant and sank her savings into making a salon. She hired the former vegetarian war orphan to cut hair and Miss Connon's cousin to do perms and coloring. The salon immediately took off and forever after the granny referred to it as "my business enterprise" as if it were General Electric or something. But we all forgave her that because you could get really good haircuts there.

When the former vegetarian war orphan cut his own hair, getting rid of the dreads and his beard, he turned out to be quite handsome underneath. One day Miss Connon came in to get her hair cut and (this is the part I love), *he asked her out.*

Uncle Jack and I were having dinner one night at The Girl on the Red Swing when they came in. "What's to come of that, huh?" he said, winking at me and picking marshmallows out of his clam chowder.

The B and B really took off and it kept Kate hopping because she mostly ran it while Uncle Jack continued with real estate.

Evie and Bert did the usual gangbusters business at The Girl on the Red Swing. Evie finally printed on the menu, "Mini Marshmallows *Optional*," because some people found it disturbing that they were in *everything*. Waffles, on the other hand, remained nonnegotiable. I think we were all glad about that.

Six months after Ked returned, Kate and Uncle Jack had a baby girl. "Eleven more to go," Uncle Jack always teased Kate, and she always blushed. But sometimes I'd catch a glint in his eye that made me think he was partly serious too. They named their little girl Daisy. Excellent, I thought, we've got kind of a family flower thing happening here.

Two months after Daisy's birth the seer died.

It was sad, even though he'd been old and ill a long time. He didn't have much to leave. No money to speak of. He had rented his rooms. But all he did have he left to Ked.

Including his boat.

Polynesian Jell-O Salad

This is Polynesian because of the pineapple. Bring a can of pineapple tidbits, half a cup of water and one quarter cup of sugar to a boil. Add a small package of lime Jell-O and chill until it starts to gel. Fold in half a cup of whipped cream, half a cup of cottage cheese, half a cup of mini marshmallows and half a cup of nut pieces, whatever kind you like. Chill until solid.

This was the last recipe in the ill-fated *Just Throw Some Melted Butter on It and Call It a Day*. But the recipes found a new home in Coal Harbor's youth cookbook, which my mother was putting together for Fishermen's Aid. Uncle Jack's commission had had to go to help buy the mountain, so Fishermen's Aid got nothing and my mom started the cookbook drive again. Ked and I donated all our recipes and tried to credit Evie where we could because so many of them came from her. It was a bonanza for people who wanted to learn to cook with marshmallows. Of course other kids contributed too, including Eleanor Milkmouse (although not from her family's ultravaluable six-hundred-year-old file). After her recipe she appended a list of seventeen ways to chop without using a sharp instrument. Oh, it just *drove me crazy!*